The Fifth Man

The Fifth Man

James LePore

THE
STORY PLANT

The Story Plant
The Aronica-Miller Publishing Project, LLC
P.O. Box 4331
Stamford, CT 06907

Print ISBN-13: 978-1-61188-065-6
E-book ISBN-13: 978-1-61188-066-3

Visit our website at www.thestoryplant.com

First Story Plant Printing: February 2013

Printed in The United States of America

To the memory of my cousin Maria Fuccello, whose joyful and vibrant love I miss every day.

ACKNOWLEDGMENTS

Many thanks to my friends Greg and Joy Ziemak, Tom and Monique Molesky, Julia Macklin and Mike Montera for helping me do research in Brighton Beach. Also to an Iraq veteran friend who wishes to remain anonymous for his weaponry expertise. I am grateful as always to my friend and editor Lou Aronica. He knows what's missing and how to get it out of me. Last but not least I am grateful to Karen, the First Angel, for all she does to support me. Thank God I met her.

Before all else, be armed.

– Niccolo Machiavelli

PROLOGUE

Manhattan, January 19, 2005, 4:00 p.m.

Chris Massi, a surgical bandage across the bridge of his nose, his left arm in a sling, pulled up the collar of his wool coat with his free hand and looked down at the pit where the twin towers once stood, then up at the sky, which was dull and gray and starting to spit snow. Next to him, leaning over the concrete parapet, stood a man he knew only as Mr. White and had only met once before.

"We appreciate what you did," said Mr. White.

"You're welcome," Chris replied. "I'm sorry I couldn't get an answer."

"We rarely get answers in this business," Mr. White said. "Tell me about your contact in the restaurant."

"I only made it to the foyer. Two young guys, in their twenties, Russian, met me."

"Can you give us a sketch? We do it by computer now."

"Sure."

"Then what?"

"They told me I was going to get my wish, I was going to meet with a representative of Bratva Mafya. They blindfolded me, took me out a back entrance and put me in a car. You know where they took me."

"Who did they send?"

"You mean the Bratva guy?"

"Yes."

"I don't know. A man with a gravelly voice. Middle aged. Sarcastic. I think he walked with a limp."

"Why do you say that?"

"His gait sounded uneven on the concrete floor. It's a guess."

"He spoke English?"

"With a heavy Russian accent."

"What did he say?"

"He said hello, and then the bomb went off, or whatever it was."

"It was a grenade. Then what?"

"I was thrown from my chair. My shoulder hit something hard. A stack of metal pallets. They toppled over on me. One was on my chest and face. I was on my back. I came to with both of my eyes filled with blood. The blindfold had come off. I heard voices and footsteps. I just lay there, pretending I was dead. Someone lifted the pallet away and shone a flashlight in my face.

I could see the light pass across my eyes. Then he spit in my face."

"Spit in your face? Did he say anything?"

"Sicilian scum."

"Sicilian scum. That doesn't sound like a pro to me. How many were there?"

"Two."

"Did they say anything else?"

"Dead. The other one said dead."

"That's it?"

"Yes."

"Then what?"

"I heard a grunting sound. Then there were footsteps and a gun shot."

"They shot a survivor."

"That's what I figured. I can't believe I'm alive."

"Your two Mafya men took most of the shrapnel. You were lucky."

"Was it meant for me?"

"We don't think so. Did you see them at all?"

"The blood was starting to coagulate, to thicken, and I was still bleeding, but I managed to open my eyes. I saw them walking toward a door. When they got to it, one of them turned to look at me. He had his gun out. There was an exit light above the door, red, so I could see his face in the red glare."

"What did he look like?"

"Feral—a snout nose, slanted eyes like a wolf. Going bald."

"Did he see *you*? I mean, did he realize you were alive?"

"I don't know. The room was filled with smoke and dust from the explosion. An alarm went off. He froze for a second, then the other one pulled him by the arm and they fled."

"Did you see the other one?"

"No, he wasn't under the exit sign. Too dark, too smokey."

"I'm sorry to have left you on your own like that."

Chris shrugged. He knew what the deal was going in. No backup, no gimmicks. "Do you know anybody matching that description?" he asked.

Mr. White did not answer immediately. He took out a small sterling silver flask, unscrewed the cap carefully and took a sip. "Care for some?" he said, offering the flask to Chris. "It's Armagnac, a hundred and ten years old."

Chris was cold. He had been released from the hospital that morning. His head and his dislocated shoulder still ached. The wounds from the shrapnel that had lodged in his left leg were still raw. He took the flask and drank, glad that he did when he felt the liquor hit his stomach and almost immediately spread to the ragged ends of his central nervous system.

"So," he said, handing back the flask. "What happened?"

"It was probably an internal Odessa Mafya thing. A betrayal, an order disobeyed."

Chris shrugged. He was familiar with Mafia executions.

"There *is* something else, though," said Mr. White.

Chris waited, wondering what was coming.

"The Russians," Mr. White continued, "have deeply clandestine units, just as we do. There are rumours about one headed by an agent who looks like a wolf. They say he came out of the Odessa Mafia, or maybe he infiltrated it for some reason."

"Rumours? Anything about 9/11?"

"Yes, but just rumours, wild talk in the Middle East."

"About what?"

"That Bin Laden had a wolf for an ally, that a Russian wolf visited Bin Laden at his camp in Kunar Province, that the wolf provided finances. The Islamists hate dogs, but this wolfman inflamed their imagination at the time."

"So maybe that was him, my feral looking bald friend."

"It's probably a myth. They're big on Messianic myths, the fanatics. Still, I'd like you to help with a sketch of him too. You can help us put a face to the rumours. Someday a match may turn up."

"And then what?" Chris said. "I'd like to meet the wolfman on my own terms."

"No, I'm sorry, but that you cannot do."

"Don't you want an answer?"

"I'm told we no longer do, that it was farfetched to think the Russians were involved in 9/11."

"What do *you* think?"

"I think they were. Look where we are, bleeding in two wars. The Middle East street hates us. Just where they want us."

"But nobody's listening."

"Correct. They tell me the Cold War's over, the Russians are no longer ambitious, they want to co-exist with us, blah, blah."

Chris smiled. "Did I pass my test?"

"Yes. I'm authorized to consummate our deal."

"You know my terms."

"I do, but all you'll have is my word."

"You're being videotaped right now. With audio."

"Is that a joke?"

Chris shrugged. "You have my word, too."

The footprint of the trade center, starkly naked, had remained untouched in the last four years while New York politicians and businessmen fought over turf and money, as only New York politicians and businessmen could. The *pezzi da novante,* Chris's father used to call them, *big shots,* living like kings, their hands in everyone's pockets, above the law. *Make your own law* he had said to him many times. *Make your own law and live by it.* Little did Joe Black Massi know that one day the most powerful people in the country—the very epitome of the *pezzi da novante*—would be carving out a kingdom for his son, Chris, where his word would indeed be law.

Mr. White, in his mid-sixties, his face rugged and lined with age and high in color, his eyes a twinkling blue-gray, smiled. "I have been thinking of retiring," he said. "But not now. This project is for me the ultimate opportunity."

Chris nodded and remained silent.

"I don't exist of course."

Chris said nothing.

"A man named Max French will be joining us in a few minutes," Mr. White said. "He's an oddball, an outlier, but a pro. If you agree, he will be your right hand."

"Will *he* exist?"

"Yes." Mr. White smiled again. "One more thing," he said.

"Yes?"

"I think this wolfman was coming over to make sure you were dead, to shoot you. Now he'll be wondering if you saw his face."

"That sounds right."

"That makes things different. You can back out if you want."

The snow was coming down heavier now, and a man in his mid-forties with short sandy hair, his hands in the pockets of his overcoat was walking toward them.

"You mean," Chris said, "if he's this super-secret spy, he'll want me dead because I can identify him?"

"Yes."

"How about another drink?" Chris said. "To seal our deal."

Mr. White had put the flask back in his inside coat pocket. He drew it out now, unscrewed the cap, took a swig, and handed it to Chris, who took a deep drink.

"No," Chris said, handing the flask back, remembering the wolfman's saliva on his face, imprinting the memory on his brain. "I'm in."

"Good," Mr. White said. "Here comes Max French. I'll leave you now. Good luck. Max will know how to reach me."

1.

Manhattan, Monday, August 20, 2012, 4:00 p.m.

Dear Mr. Massi,

The storage unit named above is due for renewal on September 1. The tenant, Mr. Joseph Massi, left instructions directing us to notify you of the renewal date in the event that he himself did not renew by July 31. Mr. Massi has not renewed. We have various renewal programs available. If you do not wish to renew, you must clean out the unit by no later than August 20. Please advise as to your wishes.

Sincerely,
Anna Cavanagh, Manager

Matt Massi read this short letter standing in the kitchen of his mother's co-op on Manhattan's Upper East Side. His mother, Theresa, was in the living room on the phone. He looked at the date on the letter, August 1, and then at the postmark on the envelope, also August 1. Theresa's prior address in New Jersey was crossed out and her New York address written under it. The word *Forward* and a red arrow pointing to the New York address were stamped next to it.

He pulled his cell phone out of the front pocket of his jeans, found the number of Wall Storage at the bottom of Anna Cavanagh's letter and dialed it.

"Wall Storage," a woman said, after only one ring.

"Is this Anna Cavanagh?" Matt asked.

"Yes it is."

"Hi. My name is Matt Massi. I got a letter from you about a storage unit. My uncle's unit, Joseph Massi."

"I did not think you would call." Matt did not respond. There was something about Anna Cavanagh's deep voice that, despite her sexy accent, bothered him. A wariness. As if she didn't trust him for some reason, though of course they'd never met. Weird. *Too serious.*

"Do you want to renew?" she said.

"I don't know."

"I will close in an hour. The contract is terminated today. You have to decide now."

"What's the shortest I can renew for?"

"Six months is the minimum. Plus one month security."

"How much?"

"Twenty-one hundred dollars."

"Now?"

"Yes. On a six month contract, you are required to pay it all at once."

I am *required*, Matt thought, *all at once*, trying to mimic the formal, metronomic way she spoke, as if she were picturing each word in her head before sounding it out. Each word an experiment. What *was* that accent? And what kind of face and body matched it?

"Fine," he answered, finally.

"I will need your credit card."

"Hold on." Matt slipped his wallet out of his back pocket. "How do I get in, by the way?"

"To the unit?"

"Yes."

"Do you have a key?"

"No."

"You have to call a locksmith. Tell him there is an industrial lock on it. A puck lock. If there is damage to the door, we will charge to your credit card."

"Who's *we*?"

"Please?"

"Do you work for a company or is this your place?"

"That's not...that's none of your business."

Matt had fished his Visa card from his wallet and was staring at the number. Anna's tone had softened slightly when she realized she was about to make a quick twenty-one hundred dollars, but then hardened again when he asked his last question. How old was she? Twenty? Thirty? And why so serious? So grave? If she looked anything like she sounded—cold, suspicious, bitter even—she wasn't pretty. Still, there *was* that accent, and that husky voice.

∧ ∧ ∧ ∧ ∧

"Who was that?" Theresa asked, when he clicked off. She was in the kitchen now, near the built-in desk where she paid bills and kept her cookbooks, going through her purse.

"The bookstore."

"At Columbia?"

"Yes. I need to read five books in the next two weeks. They're sending them here." He had actually been on the phone with the Columbia Bookstore before calling Wall Storage, while his mother was in her bedroom getting herself ready to go out.

"Did you get your mail?" Theresa asked, her keys in her hand.

"Yes."

She looked at him now, her head slightly tilted.

"What was that letter from the storage company?" she asked.

"Uncle Joseph stored some things and put my name on the papers."

"What things?"

"I don't know."

"Down the shore? He hated the beach."

Matt did not reply. The people that had known his father's younger brother, Joseph Massi, Jr., all said he looked just like him—black hair swept away from the forehead and falling in waves below the ears, piercing, dark brown eyes—the irises so uniformly dark you had to look hard to see a pupil—a straight, proud nose, thick sensuous lips...Matt was the last Massi to see Joseph alive.

"He's been dead eight years," Theresa continued.

"I know."

"Are you going down there?"

"I renewed the contract. I'll go down next week."

Matt could see that his mother wanted to say more. He was twenty-two, about to re-enter Columbia, to start his senior year. He had spent the last twelve months in Ukraine and Turkey, working for a shipping company owned by a friend of his father's, a client. A lot of those twelve months he had spent on a Greek-registered oil tanker going back and forth through the Bosporus and the Dardanelles, bringing Russian oil from Odessa to a half-dozen Mediterranean ports. Thanks to his bunkmate, and the crew at large, he now spoke semi-fluent Greek and could get by in a seaman's rough Russian. He was grown up, but that wasn't what stopped Theresa. It was their history, the things that happened eight years ago, the things that brought them to where they were now. Their relationship had mended, but he had defied her then, when he was fourteen, had wrested himself from her control. Had she forgiven him? Had he forgiven her?

"Do you like the apartment?"

"It's great, Mom."

"Did you call your grandfather?"

"Yes."

"Tom's son lives in the building."

"Tom Stabile?"

"Yes."

"You didn't tell me."

"What's the difference?"

"Mom..." Matt did not dislike Tom Stabile, Theresa's husband. Nor did he like him. His reaction to Stabile was an easy neutrality that infuriated his mother.

"Have I been disrespectful?"

"No, you haven't, but I know what you're thinking."

"No, you don't."

Theresa stared at him.

"Who else lives there?" he asked.

"Ally Scarpa's the super."

"Nick's son? You're kidding. He's out of jail?"

"Yes." Theresa raised her eyebrows as she said this, stopping for a click at the top before lowering them, a movement that, combined with a slight tightening of the lips, transmitted a wordless mother-to-son message that Matt had received and acknowledged, sometimes silently, sometimes not, countless times.

"It's a Mafia-fest over there," he said, deciding to make this one of the non-silent times.

"Grandpa owns the building. What did you expect?"

Matt said nothing, but he smiled, and shook his head, acknowledging to his mother, who stood before him proudly, still striking at forty-six, that what bound them most profoundly, besides their blood, was their membership by birth in an old-fashioned mob clan, a Mafia family that few knew existed, but that, deft and imaginative, swam quietly with the deadliest and most powerful of sharks in the commercial seas of the twenty-first century.

"You have your Uncle Joseph's smile," Theresa said, staring at him, her eyes softening. "What do you think's in the locker?"

"Heroin, cocaine, crystal meth. Stolen televisions."

"Stop it."

They both smiled now, and Matt could see from the look in his mother's eyes that she was thinking of Joseph, remembering him, the bad Massi brother, the heroin addict, who, he had come to realize, she may have loved more than the one she married.

"Where are you off to?" he asked.

"Shopping with Dana Carbone, then dinner someplace. Join us."

"Maybe; I'm picking a friend up at LaGuardia. I'll call you."

That look again. That almost imperceptible tilt of the head and narrowing of the large brown DiGiglio eyes. *A friend? What kind of friend? Male? Female? LaGuardia?*

"It's the guy from the *Scorpion,*" Matt said, smiling, giving his mother a break. "Nico. I told you about him. He's coming over to visit relatives."

"Oh. Okay. Bring him to dinner."

"I'll call you."

2.

Brighton Beach, Brooklyn, August 20, 2012, 7:00 p.m.

"This is quite a place," Matt said. He had been looking around Sabrina's—the Russian restaurant cum nightclub on the boardwalk in Brighton Beach—while Nico was in the back talking to his cousin, one of the owners.

"You like it?"

"What's not to like?"

"The girls?"

"They're beautiful."

Nico was referring to the two young women in gold bikini tops and sequin-covered skirts who were dancing under blue and red strobe lights on a raised platform on the stage in the restaurant's large main room. The jagged-edged skirts revealed a lot of leg, and seemed somehow, Matt noticed, to reveal a bit more as the girls waved to Nico and smiled when he passed the stage on his way to the kitchen. He and Matt were seated outside at a front corner table on a covered patio facing the beach. The Atlantic Ocean, solemn and calm tonight under a cloudless sky, lay just fifty yards beyond. Through open-air doors behind them, they had a view of the noisy interior. The dancers had been joined by a singer in a low-cut sequin dress that matched her golden hair and their sparkling outfits. She was smiling and waving at the people at one of the tables near the stage. Her teeth, Matt noticed, were very white and beautiful and her lipsticked lips bright red.

"The singer is also my cousin."

Matt nodded and smiled. He had spent long stretches at sea with the twenty-five year old Nico, and heard a lot about his so-called cousins. In Odessa, it paid apparently to be a part of a large family with plenty of *nerodnoy brat*.

"You don't believe me?"

"Sure I do."

"Later, I will prove it. We both have flowers on our asses."

"Tattoos?"

"*Nyet*. Birthmarks. In the shape of a poppy, the Ukrainian flower."

"Is the vodka good here?" Matt asked.

"Matvey! This you do not have to ask."

He didn't. The vodka, brought out especially for them in tall bottles without labels—a family recipe according to Nico—was the best he ever had, silky smooth with an earthy bite and a clean, happy aftertaste, leaving you wanting more. Which Matt, who could hold his liquor, did and did not. He paced himself, and the food— brought out endlessly by waiters in white shirts and black bowties, who spoke rapid-fire Russian to Nico—helped him stay relatively sober. He had spent more than a few nights in ports from Sebastopol to Palermo drinking with Nico, who never got drunk. After ten vodkas his boyish face might turn a deep red and he might smile a lot, but that was it. He greased six-inch cables, wrestled with tie-down hardware and scraped rust all day onboard ship, and was tall and tanned and very strong. One night in Naples he tossed around some locals like they were ragdolls. They had called him a dumb Polack, a double insult. Matt wasn't worried though, about anything Nico might or might not do. He just never got drunk with strangers, or in public.

After dinner, they sat on the boardwalk and smoked Nico's black market Turkish cigarettes while they waited for the last show to end, when the singer and one of the dancers were supposed to join them and continue the evening.

"Why are you here, Nick?" Matt asked. They were facing the sea, the better to catch the faint breeze drifting in from Ireland, the night still hot and humid.

"To visit my family," Nico answered. "To play in America."

"That's all?"

"No, there is more, but if I tell you what it is, you will be...What do I mean to say? A participant?"

"Then don't tell me."

"I agree. I will not. May I ask you, Matt, who are you?"

Matt smiled and glanced over at the young Ukrainian, who had his thickly muscled arms stretched out on the back of the bench they were sitting on, some few feet apart. Their eyes met for a second, and then both looked out to sea. Such patience, he thought, *a year at sea.*

"I'm a college student," Matt replied, flinging his half-smoked cigarette over the metal rail in front of him, watching it land and die out on the sand below. "I told you."

"American college students do not get visas to work on oil tankers on the Black Sea."

"The Scorpion was Greek."

"And your father is really a lawyer?"

"Yes, The Piraeus Group is a major client."

"Not Mafia?"

"The Mafia doesn't exist any more, Nick, except in the movies."

"Our captain must watch the American movies."

"What did he say?"

"Nothing was to happen to you."

"Why are you bringing this up now? You had a year to bring it up."

"I only take orders."

"Yes, I understand. Who from?"

"Gods in tall buildings. Men in kitchens drinking vodka." *Wawdka,* was how he pronounced it. It made Matt smile.

"So, why are you here?"

"I am to ask if you are interested in a business proposition."

Matt took his time replying. This meant that Nico's people knew at least that money was a part of Matt's world. And possibly—likely—more. How much more? For Nico to ask a question like this of Matt Massi was to take the risk that the tall, open-faced young Russian would not return from America, that he would never be heard from again.

"Someone has done some research," Matt said, finally.

"That goes both ways, I'm sure," Nico said.

"No, Nick, we're friends," Matt replied. "But it could always be done now." Even if your last name is not Pugach, and you were not born in Kiev, and your mother was not the woman who fed us dinner on the roof of her apartment building last summer, I could find out who you are in a couple of hours. And I will.

3.

Jackson, New Jersey, August 21, 2012, 3:00 p.m.

"I need to rent another unit," Matt said. He had rung the bell at the counter and waited several minutes for Ms. Cavanagh, she of the great accent and the chip on her shoulder, to appear. He spent those minutes looking around the Wall Storage office, which was neat and clean, but sad, its two faux leather and faux chrome chairs against a side wall, a Walmart flower print hanging slightly askew above them; a faux leather sofa under the room's one window. And it was hot, near ninety degrees in the room. The air conditioner fitted into a wall cutout sat there silently, the words old and broken written all over it. While he was waiting a fax came in, something, he could not miss seeing, from the Superior Court of Ocean County, Domestic Violence Unit.

"In addition to A-17?" Anna Cavanagh answered.

"Yes."

"What size?"

"Small, I just have to put this in it," said Matt, lifting the duffle bag he was holding above the level of the counter that separated them.

"I have lockers behind the office."

"So we don't have to go outside?" Matt was thinking of Nico, sitting in Matt's car in the parking lot just inside the front gate. He had walked from unit A17, the duffle bag over his shoulder, through the back streets of the facility and entered the office through a back door.

"No. We go there," Cavanagh said, pointing to a metal door to her right.

"Is there an entrance from the outside?"

"Yes, behind the office, but I will take you through from here."

"Good, let's do it."

"I will need your credit card."

Matt, twenty-two, six foot tall, a trim one hundred ninety pounds of good-looking young man untempered by any bad experience with women, had been, as a matter of course, rapidly assessing Anna Cavanagh as they spoke. After saying *let's do it,* he paused to take a better look. She was far from what he had expected. Her pinned-up hair—what he could see of it—was a pretty, golden blonde, her skin fair. A tiny bead of sweat was making its way slowly down a straight, slightly large, but finely modeled nose, a proud nose set between full lips below and wide apart green eyes above. One—the left one—was slightly off-center, looking permanently at the faint but distinct dusting of freckles on the bridge of her nose. They were beautiful, these eyes, made more beautiful by the one that was slightly cocked, but not beautiful enough to hide the shadow behind them. Of what, he could only guess. Fear? Hatred? Loss? They were eyes that would be magnetic if she ever smiled, feral if she got angry. A grown woman's eyes.

"I am waiting," said Cavanagh.

"You have it," Matt answered. Why so serious? He wanted to say, to break the ice, to get *some* kind of a reaction from her, but held back, remembering the fax he had seen. *Domestic Violence Unit.* Something was very wrong in Anna Cavanagh's life.

"I must run it through this time."

∧ ∧ ∧ ∧ ∧

In the parking lot, Nico was standing outside the car, looking toward the facility's front entrance, where the locksmith's van was just passing under the black and white gate arm. He smiled and waved when he saw Matt approaching across the hot tarmac, a smile that Matt was familiar with, beaming, wide open, too innocent to be true.

"So, what did she look like? Nasty?" Nico asked when they were underway, heading toward the Garden State Parkway. On the drive down from Manhattan, Matt had told him about his audio-based impression of Anna Cavanagh, leaving out the accent, the most interesting thing, until today, about her.

"No," Matt replied. "Worn down, wary, but not nasty."

"Good looking?"

"She's okay." She's beautiful, Matt thought. And then: *You're guarding your treasure. Like Smaug the dragon.*

"The body?"

"Tall, thin."

"Too thin? Is she a *woman*?"

"Not too thin."

"How old?"

"Twenty-nine, thirty."

"Married?"

"I don't think so."

"Twenty-nine is the best age, Matvey," Nico said. "They want to make the most of the last of their youth."

"Not this one," Matt said.

"Why not?"

"I don't know. She didn't smile once."

"For me she will smile."

"Sure, Nick, give it a try."

4.

Jackson, New Jersey, August 21, 2012, 4:00 p.m.

In the apartment behind the office, Anna Cavana-gh, laundry basket in hand, paused to take a look at herself in the pink-framed mirror in her daughter's room. She did not like thinking about her looks, not in the way she believed most women did. Was she pretty? Was she attractive to men? To *this* man, or *that* man? She had never taken more than a few steps down that path. She knew without thinking about it where it would lead her. She looked and assessed of course, but in her own way, her heart ready to cry STOP before she saw her father's smiling face, and heard his voice telling her how beautiful she was.

Now she looked a bit more carefully than usual, caution thrown tentatively to the wind, on a short leash, one might say: first at her bad eye, her ugly eye, *traumatic strabismus*, the doctor at the clinic in Prague called it. Then at her fake-looking, too-yellow hair, pinned up now against the heat, wisps of it falling on her ears and the back of a neck that seemed too long; at a face that was too angular to be pretty, the nose plain and boring and yet somehow haughty. The freckles, God, still there. Her father's face had been angular and thin, his nose large and straight and proud too, and he had been a drinker, like her husband, though she didn't know it when he was alive, living as she was in a child's dream world until that winter day in 1989.

Pretty or not, men were drawn to her; some falling for her like trees felled in a forest. *Whoosh,* and they would do anything for her. Tall, thin, her breasts large and full, her ass plump and curvy, her skin creamy, she knew what they wanted. She had learned early about sex. One of those *do-anything* men had been Skip Cavanagh, whom she married not because he begged her to, but because she could not extend her visa any longer.

Haggard was her assessment now. *Tired. Afraid.*

On her own since she was eighteen. Everyone dead. Father, mother, grandparents. Fourteen years. *America,* she thought, when she left Prague, would be the answer. There she would make a new life and find a way to forget, to put the past behind her. But she never could put it behind her, her past. She could never stop looking out that window in her little house on the outskirts of Prague. And now there was more. Reflexively, she reached to touch the bruise on her right side. Lifting her blouse, she saw that the edges were fading to an ugly yellow, that only the center was still the deep purple color of an eggplant. Today, there was no blood in her urine for the first time since Skip, drunk, high on what the cops later told her was something called crystal meth, had struck her with a baseball bat two weeks ago.

In the kitchen, she soaked a washcloth with cold water and held it first against the back of her neck and then her forehead. Through the window above the sink, she could see her son and daughter playing on the thirty-foot by thirty-foot patch of sunburned brown grass behind the building. It was sweltering hot, but, dressed for the heat in shorts and T-shirts, they seemed oblivious as they dug in the ground in the far corner near the chain-link fence that enclosed the yard. Beyond the fence a short way was the edge of the New Jersey Pine Barrens, a million acres of brush pine that surrounded her and her children and her dying little business like a monster in a dark fairy tale, ready to swallow them without warning in one quick primeval gulp.

She had immediately gone online two days ago to make sure that Matt Massi's first credit card payment had cleared. She had no doubt, having met him, that his second would be fine. Half of her units were empty and there were too many deadbeats among the other half, too many up-and-coming auctions to pay too much back rent. Matt Massi's two payments would get her through three months if she was careful. But what else would she be but careful? And then what?

In the kitchen was a television wired to the closed circuit security cameras that monitored the front gate and the storage rows on the property. The quarterly insurance bill had arrived the day after she threw Skip—with the help of the Jackson Township police and a judge who was awoken at 3:00 a.m. to sign a temporary restraining order—out. The three thousand six hundred dollar bill was still on her desk. It was either pay it or feed the kids. She checked the TV in the kitchen and the other two, in the office and in her bedroom, obsessively. Her life was in Wall Storage—all of her savings, the money she had hoarded waiting tables and tending bar for five years before she chose Frank "Skip" Cavanagh as her ticket to American citizenship. That decision had not been cold or calculated, but nevertheless she was paying a heavy price for it.

Back in the front office Anna sat at her computer and Googled Matthew Massi, finding a radio talk show host in Sacramento and a math teacher in Binghamton, New York. One fat and bald, the other thin and old. For Joseph Massi she found the same run-of-the-mill types, more of them than she expected. One was a ventriloquist in Los Angeles. This produced one of her rare smiles. Then, toward the last page of Massis, she found a 2003 New York Post article about the discovery of parts of a body in a suitcase in a canal in Brooklyn and the ensuing investigation that led to the identification of the partial corpse as that of Joseph Massi of Bloomfield, New Jersey. *The U.S. Attorney's Organized Crime Task Force surmises that Massi, a member of the Velardo crime family under suspicion of several gangland slayings, was tortured and then killed by gangland rivals in a dispute over drug territory in Brooklyn.* Below this was a brief obituary, which named Massi's surviving wife, Rose, his two sons, Christopher and Joseph, Jr., and his grandchildren Theresa and Matthew. There were no pictures.

Anna then opened the accounts folder in her hard drive and found the file for *Massi, Joseph*, whose lease was dated September 1, 2002, and whose address was listed as 15 White Oak Terrace, Bloomfield, New Jersey. In the file cabinet beneath her desk were the manila files where she kept hard copies of all of her accounts. She slid the drawer open, thumbed through until she found *Massi, Joseph* and pulled it out. Clipped to the inside cover was a copy of Mr. Massi's driver's license, which contained the photo ID required of all new lessees. There he was, Matt Massi's grandfather. An assassin. She looked for a long moment into Joseph Massi's somber, black eyes. She had not yet owned Wall Storage when he rented his unit and so had never met him face-to-face, but she had no doubt he was the real thing, and that his duffle bag held something of grave importance.

What was it? Human bones? Drugs? A million dollars? Another smile. *A close look in the mirror, a couple of smiles. An internet search.* Matt Massi had done this. The young and handsome Matt Massi, with his dark, grave eyes, thick black hair and confidant smile. And his attitude, one she had not come across before, the air of royalty about him, of a prince born to be a king.

Her thoughts turned from the Massi family to the one she used to have, and from there to the metal box in the bottom drawer of her desk, where she kept the yellowing photographs of her parents and grandparents that were all that remained of her past. She retrieved the box, opened it, and picked up the top picture of her and her father and Chessa together on their porch in the summer of 1988, taken by her grandmother. She remembered clearly, like it was yesterday, the day it was taken and, as she stared, her mind drifted to another day, the one in 1989 when she was ten years old and her life changed forever.

Her father's old Skoda would not start that morning. It was too far for her to walk to school, and so she was there, in her small second floor bedroom, to hear the hissing of a car on the road that led to her house. Had her father called a neighbor to take her to school? Looking out her window, she saw him splitting wood in the snow-covered front yard, her German Shepherd, Chessa, helping him bring logs to the pile on the front porch. The long black car, the largest she had ever seen, stopped in front of her house. A tall, handsome man, his short hair blond like hers, but with a widow's peak, got out and walked toward her father. Chessa stiffened and growled and the man drew a pistol from the pocket of his long overcoat and shot her. The rest was a blur, but a blur imprinted on her psyche as if with a chisel on stone: her father raising his arms high, turning to look up at her, staring directly into her eyes before being pushed into the car, the sound of her shoes on the steps as she ran downstairs and then outside, the car receding in the distance, Chessa lying on her side in the snow, breathing hard and fast, taking her last look at the world—at Anna—before she died. Anna's yellow hair standing on end, her scalp tingling in the cold winter air.

Anna stared at the photograph. She did not know until much later that her father had been part of the underground resistance against the police state the Soviets had imposed on his homeland. In the box was a letter from Václav Havel to her grandparents.

"We have confirmed that your son, Antonin, died in Karvina Prison in March, 1989. He was tortured and killed by the StB for his lifelong efforts to dislodge the Soviet yoke from the neck of our people..."

Anna slipped the photograph back into the metal box and returned the box to its drawer. The children had come in. She could hear them getting drinks in the kitchen where, on the floor, despite her determined efforts, a faint shadow of the blood stain from Skip's head wound remained visible. She touched her side again, remembering the blow she took from the bat, and the second swing he took, slipping and missing her and hitting his forehead on the corner of the kitchen island. He'll be back, she thought, fear for herself and her children replacing memories of her father. *He's lost his mind.* This time, I will be ready.

5.

Manhattan, August 21, 2012, 6:00 p.m.

Matt had shut his cell phone down for the ride to and from the Jersey shore. He turned it on when he got to his apartment on Carmine Street, a spacious five-room fourth-floor walkup that could house a small family and that his mother had furnished for him before his return from Europe—a bedroom, a study, a full kitchen, a living room/dining room combo, built-in bookshelves in all of the rooms, even the kitchen, many of them lined with the books Theresa had been storing for him at her big house in Jersey before she moved to Manhattan. When he turned his phone on, he was surprised to see a message from Natalya, the singer at Sabrina's. "Matvey, Nico gave me your number. I hope you don't mind. That was a lot of fun, Matvey. Please call me. We will do it again. Also, can you please erase the picture? Very embarrassing."

They had drunk *wawdka* in Natalya's apartment above Sabrina's, and played music from her collection, dancing to the Ronettes and the Rolling Stones in her small living room. Before the night was over, Nico and Natalya had revealed their birthmarks, ass cheeks side-by-side. Matt had snapped a picture with his iPhone. He laughed now, remembering the proud smiles on their faces as they looked at him over their shoulders, mooning him in tandem. They may not be who they said they were, but they were a lot of fun. And Natalya, a brunette under her blonde wig, was a knockout with a sweet face and an even sweeter body. Now she was calling him.

Matt took a shower and when he came out he dressed and then dialed a number that he knew would not be answered. He opened the package of books that had arrived from the Columbia bookstore and began browsing as he waited for a return call. *Modern Times*, by Paul Johnson; *The Road to Serfdom*; Robert Conquest, Milton Friedman. Ivy League orthodoxy did not interest Matt. A double major, in history and economics, he was in a one-on-one honors program in which he was free to read, and write, as he wished. His mentor, the head of the history department, had promised to have his collected papers published, but Matt knew he would not allow it when the time came. The ringing of his cell phone broke into his thoughts abruptly.

"Dad," he said, after sliding the unlock bar and pushing the speaker feature on his phone.

"Matt."

"There's something you need to know," Matt said, getting right to the point, hoping he had done the right thing in calling this particular number.

"Hold on, Matt," his father said, his voice light, even teasing. "First, how are you?"

"Good. Fine. School starts in two weeks."

"And your mom?"

"She's fine. She went a little overboard furnishing my apartment. We're having dinner tonight."

"Tess?"

"She's joining us."

"She's coming over here for a few days."

"She told me."

Matt had been nervous waiting for his father's call. He had dialed this number only once before, when he was sixteen and had finished last in the mile event in a high school track meet. His father had admonished him then. *This number is not for hurt pride, Matt.* Now he seemed breezy, unconcerned. *Gods in tall buildings,* Nico's phrase, came to Matt's mind, though he knew that the metaphor was not quite accurate when it came to his father, who might *own* tall buildings, but did not, as far as Matt knew, have an office in one.

"What's up?" Chris Massi asked.

"Two things."

"Go ahead."

"I got a letter from a self-storage place at the shore. I thought it was Uncle Joseph's, but it was Grandpa Joe's. Dad, there was two million dollars in it in a duffle bag."

Silence, in which Matt could hear the humming of his new refrigerator and his own quiet breathing as he pictured his father in his office on the top floor of that crazy old house in Piraeus.

"What did the letter say?" Chris Massi asked, finally.

"What letter?"

"The one from the storage company."

"That Joseph Massi had pre-paid the rent for ten years, that if he didn't renew I was to be contacted."

"It's old man Velardo's money."

"The Boot?"

"Yes."

"What should I do with it?"

"It's yours. Whatever you want."

"Mine?"

"There were rumors about this money, Matt. I never knew if they were true or not. Now I do. Your grandfather was holding it for the old man, but he's dead and so is most of his family that matters. It's the spoils of war. Joe Black obviously wanted you to have it."

"There was no note, Dad. Just the cash."

"He wasn't much of a letter writer, my father."

"Dad..."

"It's your money, Matt."

"What should I do with it?"

"Think of it as a test."

"A test?"

"Yes, you passed the first part. You told me."

"What's the second part?"

"What you do with the money."

"Dad?"

"Yes."

"I don't want the money."

Silence at the other end. And then: "Your grandfather left it to you, Matt."

"Why?"

"He must have had his reasons."

Matt had lived with his father in Manhattan from 2003 to 2007, while he went to high school. Except for a handful of Chris's short absences, and the weekends Matt occasionally spent with his mother in New Jersey, they had had dinner and conversation together every night during those years. As a consequence, Matt had learned to read his father's silences, so he knew for a fact what this last one meant.

"What's the second thing, Matt?"

Matt paused for a second before answering. Two million dollars. Fuck. Most people would be ecstatic, but Matt was not most people. He saw the money as a burden, not a blessing. And then there was the oddness of the situation, his father's matter-of-fact tone, as if...as if *what*? But his father had moved on. That part of the conversation—the part where he might have an opportunity to complain or make a joke or ask for advice—was over. That's what his father's silence had meant.

"One of my shipmates is here," Matt said, finally. "The Russian guy I told you about, Nico."

"Nico Pugach."

"Yes."

"What about him?"

"He wants to sell me some diamonds."

"Are you interested?"

This question stopped Matt in his tracks. *Are you interested?* Later, when the Nico Pugach affair was over and done, he would realize exactly what the question was and what his father had meant it to be: a turning point, a choice to make.

"Should I be?" he replied, slightly stunned, but without hesitation. "He says I would have the contacts to re-sell them for a huge profit."

"So he thinks he knows who you are."

"Yes."

"Does he know about the two million?"

"No."

"Does anybody?"

"No. Well..."

"Well what?"

"I had to get a locksmith. There was a padlock on the duffle bag as well that needed to be sheared off. He saw the top layer of cash."

"That's not good."

"I know. When he left, I rented another unit and put the duffle bag in it."

"Good, that's it? Nobody else?"

"No, no one else knows."

"Keep it that way."

"Of course."

"Did Nico mention a price? Any details?"

"Five hundred thousand. He said they're worth ten million retail, several million or more to a middle man."

"When are you seeing him?"

"Later tonight."

"Tell him you'll think about it. Call me at this number tomorrow at this time. If I don't call you back, call again the next night at the same time. Keep doing that until I *do* call you back."

"Okay."

"Matt."

"Yes."

"Be careful of this Nico. From now on only meet him in public places, always someplace you know. Don't go anyplace alone with him, not even in a car or taxi. Understand?"

"Yes, Dad."

"Anything else?"

"I have a question."

"Go ahead."

"Is this why you made me take a year off from college?"

More silence. His father, like a Zen master, a very incongruous Zen master, had said to him many times, *take everything at face value, take nothing at face value.* He had puzzled over this obviously contradictory advice for years, until Nico showed up in America and seemed so different—and then asked him for half a million dollars.

"That's a good question. And you know what I say about questions."

"They're the royal road to consciousness."

"Yes."

"I learned last semester you stole that from Freud. Sort of. He said it was *dreams* that are the royal road to consciousness."

Chris Massi laughed his deep throaty laugh, a sound that filled Matt with happiness because it was so rarely that he heard it.

"We'll talk about Freud when I see you."

"When will that be? Are you still coming home in two weeks?"

"Maybe not," his father replied. "But you may have to come here. We'll see."

"Of course."

"You understand what I'm saying about Nico, Matt? You'll be careful?"

"I will."

"Good."

"Dad."

"Yes."

"What about my question?"

"The world is a dangerous place, Matt. Most people delude themselves into thinking otherwise. I wanted you to see it for yourself."

"Dad, did you see this coming? From Nico?"

"It's nothing, Matt. Nothing that can't be handled."

Nothing and everything, Matt thought, thinking like his father, surprising himself.

6.

Manhattan, August 21, 2012, 8:00 p.m.

"That's a heck of a climb," Tess Massi said.

"It's free and it's safe," Matt replied.

"Is that what Mom said?"

"Who else? Look around. I get off the plane, I go to her apartment, she gives me the keys, and here I am."

"Except for the four flights, it's perfect."

Brother and sister, sitting across from each other on plush easy chairs, looked around at Matt's living room. It *was* perfect: subdued, masculine, the furniture solid and handsome, an oversized, ruby-colored Persian rug on the newly polished hardwood floor anchoring it all with quiet elegance.

"Does the fireplace work?" Tess asked.

"Mom says it does."

"I'm surprised there's no piano."

Matt smiled. He and Tess had been forced by Theresa to take weekly piano lessons for several years on the Steinway in Theresa's demi-mansion in New Jersey.

"It'll probably just show up," Matt said. "She'll hire a crane to get it up here."

"Along with Mrs. Pescatore," Tess said. "Remember those pinches? The black and blue marks?"

"Jesus, Tess, I was thirteen."

"Shocking, feeling up your fifty-year-old piano teacher. You're lucky she just pinched you."

"I think I have permanent muscle damage," Matt said, grabbing his right bicep with his left hand, smiling, remembering the wide-bodied Mrs. Pescatore, how he had trembled with her heavy breasts so near. Trembled and, unbelievably, touched.

"How are you doing," Tess asked.

"Good."

"I'm jealous."

"Why?"

In the pause that followed, Matt eyed his sister. Two years older, raven-haired, her eyes big and luminous, an A student, mature beyond her years, confident. She had been their father's favorite, a thought that still hurt but, thank God, not too badly anymore.

"Well," Tess answered, "*I* would like to have done it."

"What?" Matt said. "Spent a year on an oil tanker? I worked ten hours a day, fourteen when I had the watch. You saw the pictures I sent you, where I slept, who I bunked with. Are you kidding?"

"I mean *chosen*."

"Chosen?" Matt had never found it easy to get a good read on Tess's interior life. Now he was slightly stunned. Had the wheel turned?

"Yes, Matt," Tess said, "*chosen. By Dad*."

"You would never have lasted."

"I don't mean to do what you did."

"Then what?"

"Teo..."

"Tess."

"Do you know what Dad does?"

"What he *really* does?"

"Yes."

"I'm not stupid, Tess."

"I didn't say you were. Don't be so sensitive."

"I'm not being sensitive. He took over for Grandpa. It's obvious."

"I'm not so sure."

"Tess..." Matt stopped himself. Or rather, another insight did. "Let's not go there," he said.

"That's not it," said Tess. "I know what he does. I know what Grandpa did, what Uncle Frank does."

"Then what?"

"We're missing something."

We're missing something? Despite himself, Matt felt gratified to be joining Tess in analyzing something that—and this he freely admitted to himself—he had never thought needed analyzing. His dad was who he was.

"I don't think so," he said.

"Let me put it this way, Teo: what Mafia don would send his only son to spend a year on a Greek oil tanker in the Mediterranean and the Black Sea?"

"This one did."

"There's something I'm not getting."

Back to the first person singular.

"When you find out what it is, let me know."

"I'm going to Skopelos tomorrow night on the Piraeus jet. Come with me."

"I can't."

"Why? It's Dad's birthday. School doesn't start for two weeks."

"I'm in the middle of something."

Another pause, as Matt and Tess stared at each other. Fuck, Matt thought, seeing the look in his sister's eyes. I just can't keep my mouth shut.

"For Dad?" Tess asked, finally.

"Yes."

Now Tess's eyes softened. She leaned across the empty space between them and took one of her brother's hands in hers. "I'm worried," she said.

"Why?"

"I don't know. I just am."

"Don't. I'm fine."

"Let me worry, Teo. You know what Dad always said. It's a form of prayer."

"Okay, Tess," Matt replied. "Pray for me, like you did when we were kids and I was always in trouble. You used to say, 'I'm praying for you, Teo, that you won't be an idiot forever.'"

Now they both smiled, and Matt could feel the pressure increase as Tess squeezed his hand tighter, and he could see the love in her eyes, and the fear.

7.

Piraeus, Greece, August 22, 2012, 12:30 a.m.

Chris Massi *did* own tall buildings, though not in his name, and also houses. One of these was a very modest affair, crammed in like a piece of a jigsaw puzzle among many others on a twisting street at the top of a hill overlooking the smallest of Piraeus's three harbors, Munichia. The oddly shaped three-story house's best feature was the view of the busy harbor from its top floor and rooftop deck, a sweeping vista to the north and south along the coast of the Saronic Gulf, and west out over the green Aegean, which tonight, as Chris gazed at it from his small study, was dark and quiet. The reflected lights of huge cruise ships tied to bulkheads and many smaller vessels moored within the harbor's safe confines sparkled on its placid surface like diamonds under a sheet of black glass. One of those small vessels was his, a Fleming 75 yacht, *Eleftheria*, with oversized gas tanks, a specially tooled engine and a Greek captain whose brother-in-law was Munichia's harbormaster.

Yes, Matt, Chris thought, that *is* why I asked you to take a year off from Columbia; to work on a tanker delivering the world's most important commodity to some of the world's most dangerous cities. To toughen you, and to see what kind of crowd you would attract. You were bound to attract one no matter where you were or what you were doing. Better where I could watch.

On Chris's desk was a deceptively simple but perfectly secure phone, hard-wired for him by a local employee of OTE, the largest Greek telecom provider, who moonlighted for special clients. Chris lifted the old-fashioned black plastic-covered handset from its squat base, dialed a number from memory and hung up. A few minutes later, the phone rang.

"Max," Chris said after lifting the receiver and placing it against his left ear.

"Yes, *c'est moi.*"

"Where are you?"

"Arizona."

"Doing what?"

"Helping with some training."

"I need you to go to New York. Can you?"

"When?"

"Now. As soon as possible."

"What's up?"

"I think our Russian friends have made contact."

"With Matt?"

"Yes."

"Anybody we know?"

"The Nico Pugach kid."

"Ah."

"Yes. Call me when you land. I'll fill you in."

"Just me?"

"For now. But we have friends there."

"I'm on my way."

Chris hung up and used the same phone to call *Eleftheria's* captain.

"Send the launch, Costa," he said when the captain answered. "We leave tonight."

"Tess?"

"She can fly to Skiathos on the small jet. I'll arrange it."

"Anything else?"

"Yes Costa, your friends at the Café Eleni, ask them if there's any talk of diamonds gone missing."

"Do you suspect someone?"

"No, but they're on offer, ten million dollars worth."

"It will be done."

Chris took his custom-made German binoculars from a nearby shelf, but before putting them to his eyes he looked for a moment at his reflection in the window in front of him. He would turn fifty tomorrow, which was why, ostensibly, Tess was coming over. He didn't look fifty. His hair, which he wore longer than he did ten years ago when he was fighting to save his law license, and his life, was still a lustrous black; his face, except for the pale lightning-bolt shaped scar on the bridge of his nose, had not changed much. Despite the dim outline of crow's feet that were beginning to spread east and west from the corners of his eyes, it was still a young man's face. But his eyes were not young. They had seen too much real life in the last ten years to stay young and happy looking. His father chopped up in a mob slaying, his mother dead of a broken heart, his drug-addict brother killed in the one act of bravery in his short life. He looked at his eyes and then out to the Aegean, both dark and somber, both having seen their share, as Matthew Arnold put it, of the turbid ebb and flow of human misery. Then, dismissing Arnold's deep pessimism, which he shared, he put the glasses to his face and focused on *Eleftheria*—Freedom—where the launch was being lowered by the ship's first, and only, mate, Costa Vasiliou's twenty-six-year-old son, Elias.

The Russians, Chris thought, they won't go away.

8.

Manhattan, August 22, 2012, 10:00 p.m.

"Where was your sister going in that limousine, Matvey?"

"To the airport. She's going to Greece to visit my father."

"What does she do?"

"She's in graduate school in Washington."

"Which is what? *Graduate school.*"

"Post-graduate studies. You go after college."

"For what purpose?"

"International relations. She's at Georgetown."

"She is very beautiful."

"Yes," Matt answered. "And smart."

"And forbidden, yes? *Apagorevmemos.*"

Matt smiled. He and Nico were standing on the sidewalk in front of Villa Mosconi, the family-owned and operated Italian restaurant in the West Village that he and his dad went to weekly while they were living in SoHo and he was going to La Salle Academy. Sal Visco, the restaurant's bulky unofficial bouncer, a white golf shirt stretched across his thick chest and arms, was lighting up a cigarette about ten feet away, watching a boisterous group of college kids as they passed by. The night was clear and beautiful and the Village vibrated, as it always did on warm summer nights, with the energy of the young and the restless.

"Nothing is truly forbidden, Nick."

"I mean the price too high. Is that the correct English?"

"It's close enough," Matt answered. Nico, overdressed in a dark suit and tie, had been the perfect gentleman at dinner with Theresa, her friend Dana and Tess, the picture of modesty. Too modest, Matt thought, and with more English than he wants me to believe. His boat mate, the simple, rough-hewn Russian youth, had vanished.

"Where are you headed?" Nico asked.

"I have a date with Natalya. I thought you knew."

"No. Why would I know?"

"She's your cousin. You seemed close."

"Our love lives, we do not discuss."

"Do I have your permission?"

"I am honored, but you do not need it."

"What about you?"

"Little Odessa."

They shook hands and parted and Matt went back into the restaurant.

∧ ∧ ∧ ∧ ∧

Sal flipped his cigarette away and watched Nico walk east on MacDougal Street until he turned right on Sixth Avenue and was out of sight.

9.

Jackson, New Jersey, August 23, 2012, 3:00 a.m.

Anna Cavanagh woke with a start, thinking she had heard one of the kids cry out. She sat up and listened, but there were no sounds coming from their room, only a few steps away. In the past she had often been awakened by the beep in the office that indicated that someone, using their access code, had entered the premises after hours, but this system had been shut down when she couldn't pay the alarm company's bill.

The room was hot and thick with south Jersey, late-summer humidity, its two small windows wide open. Had she heard a car? She listened carefully, but heard only crickets clattering madly. Skip had called at midnight, drunk, high, she did not know which; out on bail—*how could that be?*—and threatened to come over to *his house, his business,* to see *his kids.* She had called the police. Skip was not to come within a thousand feet of her or the kids. The police were as shocked as she was that Skip was out on bail, which had been set at fifty thousand. She was hoping it was them she heard, doing a routine patrol, and not Skip. Then a movement on the television monitor in the corner to the right of her bed caught her eye. The screen was divided into four squares for the facility's four main avenues. In the upper left quadrant, Aisle A, a car was parked and a man in a ski mask was using a metal shear to cut the lock on a unit.

Anna's friend, Dale, whom she had met when they were both tending bar at one of the Jersey shore's insane clubs, had given her an air horn that her boyfriend had stolen from the golf course where he worked. The boyfriend had installed it for her on an exterior wall with a button in the office that set it off. He had also given her a gun—a Baby Glock, he called it—which she kept on her night table. Grabbing the lightweight, polymer-coated gun, she slipped out of bed, made her way quietly to the air horn button and pushed it. The sound was deafening. Then she turned to the TV monitor in the office and saw the man with the metal shear jump into the car, back out of the aisle and pull away out of sight. A minute later she heard the crack of the front gate arm as the car crashed through it. She pushed the horn's button again for good measure, and then the earmark button on the security console on her desk. Then, realizing she was naked—it was so hot she couldn't stand even wearing panties to bed—she returned to her bedroom where she quickly dressed. Back in the office, she grabbed a flashlight and, Glock in one hand, flash-light in the other, went out to the unit that the man was trying to enter. She had a hunch which one it was, and she was right. It was A-17, Matt Massi's unit, the one he had taken the duffle bag out of.

Back in her kitchen, she put a small pot of coffee on and lit up a Marlboro Light. The first deep drag calmed her down. While the coffee brewed, she fished around in the trashcan under a counter and found today's As-bury Park Press, thinking of a front-page story she had read that morning: Local Locksmith Found Shot Dead. She knew the man, Ed Shields. He had come over to help her out when there was a lock on a deadbeat's unit that was too much for her and her small arsenal of tools. He had hit on her and she had hissed him off, but he was a decent guy and never charged her.

Had he been the locksmith who opened A-17 for Matt Massi?

10.

Jackson, August 23, 2012, 11:00 a.m.

"How did they get in?"

"They must have had your code, or someone's code."

"Why didn't you call the police?"

"I have already given them enough trouble."

"What kind of trouble?"

"Do not ask."

"You mean it's none of my business?"

"Yes."

"Don't you need a police report for your insurance company?"

Silence.

"Or don't you have insurance?"

"They did not get in. Nothing was taken."

"They?"

"There were two of them, one stayed in the car."

"Can I see the video?"

"Of course."

They were standing, as before, facing each other with the office's waist-high gray Formica-covered counter between them. The south Jersey heat wave continued unabated. It was over eighty-five degrees in the un-air-conditioned office.

"You'll have to come around," Anna said, nodding toward the swinging half-door to Matt's right. As Matt made his way into the inner space, Anna pulled two leather-covered bar stools out from under the counter. When they were both seated, she clicked on a video-camera icon on her computer screen. Matt, needing a better view of the video he was about to see, brought his stool closer to Anna's. He was wearing khaki shorts and Anna was wearing a light cotton skirt. His knee touched hers and he let it stay there for a couple of seconds before pulling it away. Anna, concentrating on the computer, did not seem to notice. Or perhaps she did.

They watched a six-inch-square frame open on the screen, first appearing as a grainy gray and then resolving into a surprisingly sharp black-and-white image of a narrow, asphalt-covered street with a one-story storage building on either side. Seconds passed, and then a late-model sedan, its headlights off, turned into the narrow street heading toward them. The car stopped and a man in a ski mask got out of the driver's side, approached a unit and went at the lock with a heavy-duty metal shear. He stopped suddenly and hustled back into the car, which he then backed rapidly and seemingly effortlessly out of the aisle, executing a quick and flawless K-turn at the open end before racing away.

The screen went gray for a second or two, and then Anna appeared, naked. Frontally and very beautifully naked, her large breasts round and high and perfectly formed, her belly slightly bulging, her crotch a thick mass of silky yellow curls on which Matt's eyes were riveted until, a second later, the screen went gray again.

"Fuck," Anna said.

"What was *that*?" Matt asked.

"I thought I hit the earmark button. I must have hit the interior office button by mistake."

"Are you blushing?"

"As *you* would be."

"Can we run through it again?"

Anna laughed at this, a rough, quick, involuntary bark of a laugh. Seeing her face light up for an instant, Matt realized he was wrong about her having a magnetic smile. What he saw was a flash of innocence, a child emerging for a split second from under the depressing layers of an adulthood that he now knew—for reasons he could not explain, except for the way she laughed and then quickly stopped—had started way too early.

"I mean it," he said, smiling himself now. "You can delete the last frame. I'd also like a copy."

"It was the middle of the night," Anna said. "It was very hot."

"Anna," Matt said. "Can I call you Anna?"

"Why not?"

"Forget it. I never saw it."

They looked at each other for a second or two, during which Matt recalled the feel of Anna Cavanagh's sweaty leg when he got too close a few minutes ago. Was she remembering it too?

"Why do you want a copy?"

"To get it enhanced."

"To try to see who it was?"

"Yes."

"He had a ski mask on."

"The other person didn't, just a baseball cap. And there's the license plate. That should be easy to read."

"There is something I must tell you."

"What?"

"What locksmith did you use?"

"A guy named Ed Shields. I found him online. Why?"

"He was killed two days ago, murdered. It was in the newspaper."

Matt shook his head, remembering Shields, how talkative he was, how friendly, how he quickly quieted when he saw what was in the duffle bag.

"Did he have a family?"

"Two kids."

"Did you know him?"

"He's been here a few times."

"What kind of guy was he?"

"What do you mean? He's been dead two days. He could not have been the one who tried to get into your unit."

Matt was silent for a second. That was as far as he would go with this line of questioning.

"Can you give me the newspaper?" he asked, finally.

"Sure."

"There's something else," Matt said.

"Yes? Tell me."

"I'd like to send someone to hang out around here for a few days. Would that be okay?"

"Hang out?"

"Watch the place."

"Am I in danger?"

"You could be. Do you have a gun by any chance?"

"Yes, but I have never fired it."

"Sleep with it."

"What about my kids. I have two kids."

"Can you send them someplace?"

"I have a friend. How long?"

"A few days, a week. I'm sorry, but it's best."

Anna was silent for a moment.

"What are you thinking?" Matt asked.

"My friend has children they can play with."

"Good."

"I know who you are," Anna said. She stared at him, and as she did her bad eye seemed to be trying hard to align itself with the good one. Trying but not succeeding.

"You do?" Matt replied, matching the seriousness of her voice. "Who am I?"

"The grandson of a Mafia hit man."

Matt smiled. "Hitt Mann," was what she said, capitalized, as if she thought it was a proper noun.

"That's true," he replied. "Who are you?"

"Look around."

"Look around?"

"Yes. This is me. This place that I am losing."

"Do you have a husband?"

"Yes, but not for long."

"A boyfriend?"

"No."

"Where are you from? What is that accent?"

"Czech. I am Czech."

"Are you having trouble with your husband? I saw the domestic violence papers on your fax."

"He wants to kill me."

"Is that why you have the gun?"

"Yes."

"Can I send someone down?"

Silence again, the cocked eye again straining against itself, a sign, Matt was to eventually learn, of Anna forgetting herself as she concentrated.

"What choice do I have?" she said finally. "I cannot shut down. I have to stay in business."

"His name is Sal Visco," Matt said, thinking *what business?* "He's a gentleman. He'll be here tonight. He'll bring a cot. He can sleep in the office."

"It gets very hot in here at night."

"He'll survive."

"You must tell me what is in the duffle bag. I have a right to know."

Matt did not answer. He took a moment to look around, as if complying with what Anna had just asked him to do. Gazing up, he noticed for the first time a fan, motionless, hanging from the center of the room's ceiling.

"Why don't you turn that on?" he asked, nodding upward.

"It is broken."

Matt took his wallet from the back pocket of his shorts and pulled out ten hundred dollar bills. "Take this," he said, putting the bills on the counter. "Get the fan fixed. For Sal. The rest is for the gate out front."

Anna stared at the neat stack of money. "It's too much," she said.

"And for your trouble."

"The *duffle bag* is my trouble," Anna said. "It must be money. How much? Or drugs, like on the television. Yes? No? I have a right to know."

"I'll tell you if you call me by my name."

This brought a half smile to Anna's face. Another surprise. That was another thing Matt was starting to learn, that Anna's smiles were almost always surprises, and thus much more beautiful than ordinary smiles.

"I've seen you naked, don't forget," said Matt, seizing this small opening. "It's Matt, by the way, in case you forgot. For Matteo."

"Mott."

"Not *Mott, Matt.*"

"What do your friends call you, *Mott-Matt*?"

"Matt. My sister calls me *Teo* sometimes. To tease me."

"Tease you?"

"It's a long story. We had an Uncle Matty who we called Uncle Teo. We think he was gay, in the closet."

"How old is she, your sister?"

"Twenty-four."

"And you, how old are you?"

"Twenty-two."

"What's in the duffle bag, Teo?"

Matt smiled. "Explosives," he said. "In case someone who's not supposed to tries to open it."

"Are you serious?"

"Let's put it this way," Matt said. "If someone tries to get into that duffle bag, they're going to *wish* they had died instantly in an explosion."

11.

Manhattan, August 23, 2012, 4:00 p.m.

"The passenger has a ski mask on too, Matt, flesh colored."

"The license plate?"

"It's covered."

"They knew there'd be cameras."

"Friends of the locksmith? Someone he told?"

"Why kill him?"

"He's a witness."

"I guess so," said Matt. "What's on the baseball cap? Can you make it readable?"

"Sure. Hold on."

A few seconds later a near-perfect image of the passenger appeared on the screen, down to the fine weave of the nylon mesh of the ski mask covering the face.

"It looks like a pineapple," Matt said, staring at the yellow and blue emblem on the front of the navy blue cap.

"No, it's a soccer ball with a crown on top."

"What's it say?" Matt asked, looking at the italicized letters *YKPAIHA* spanning the middle of what he now recognized as a soccer ball.

"It's Russian. Football Federation of Ukraine."

"Thanks, Dee, I really appreciate this."

"De nada. Any time."

12.

Skopelos, August 24, 2012, 12:00 a.m.

"Who's this Diego?" Chris Massi asked.

"Diego Lopez," Max French answered. "Dee for short. He's a friend of Matt's from college."

"What does he do?"

"He's a computer geek."

"That's it?"

"He was in the same honors program as Matt. He speaks Russian, Greek, Farsi and Arabic."

Silence from Chris, then: "Are you thinking what I'm thinking?"

"Yes."

"Did you talk to him?"

"Just for a few minutes."

"Check him out."

"I will."

"Where's Matt?"

"Home on Carmine Street. I'm having an espresso across the street."

"Did he get the package?"

"I left it by his door."

"Okay. Stay with him."

"I will. Did Tess arrive okay?"

"Yes, she got here this afternoon."

"Chris?"

"Yes?"

"You know the problems. It's a big city, lot's of traffic."

"They won't touch him."

"Not if I'm around."

13.

Skopelos, August 24, 2012, 2:00 a.m.

"We have the best Retsina in the world here," Tess Massi said. "Shall I get us some?" She was slightly drunk. More than slightly, but not out of her mind, not yet.

"Of course," said Patriki, or whatever his name was. His name didn't matter. He was too handsome, his dark eyes too liquid and playful, his teeth too perfect, too white. He was too fucking sexy of a creature for his name to matter.

Tess went into the pantry that adjoined the kitchen and found a bottle of the resin wine made every year by Christina, her father's hawk-eyed housekeeper, chef and all-around major domo. Before leaving the large and well-stocked room, she took a quick look at herself in one of the pantry's glass-fronted cabinets. Her color was a glowing, reddish-brown from her three hours on the beach, her long black hair a bit frizzed from the humidity that pressed down on the island this time of year. A slight sheen of sweat remained from the dancing she and her new friend had done earlier on the waterfront deck of a local tavern but she didn't care. She knew she looked good in her simple white, side-buttoned skirt and black cotton blouse, her legs long, her body at its prime at age twenty-four. *The islands*, she said to herself, *the Aegean.* I'm free here, away from my mother, away from the pseudo-elite at Georgetown, all that Washington self-importance, all that bullshit. Why am I even doing that?

When she uncorked the wine in the kitchen, she could smell the pine resin from the local forest, which Christina said she used exclusively to seal her small oak caskets. The smell was heady, like Patriki's blend of Turkish cigarettes and subtle cologne, and the taste an acquired one. But there was no need to acquire a taste for a vagabond as handsome as Patriki. This taste she had, especially in Greece. It was her way, once or twice a year, of blowing off the pressure that seemed to be a natural part of her life in the states. Smiling, relaxed, she poured two glasses and they drank.

"Christina says she makes it the old fashioned way," Tess said, thinking, as she did, *what a silly thing to say, like a schoolgirl not knowing what to say.* I must be drunker than I thought.

"And who is Christina?"

"My father's housekeeper."

"I am going to fuck you the old fashioned way," Patriki said.

Tess had arrived on Skopelos at 3:00 p.m. and gone right to the beach with a bottle of wine on ice and a book. Back at the house she had given her father his birthday present and then napped for two hours. It had been a long day of traveling. Rested, happy to be away from what she called the New York/Washington Circle Jerk Society, she had gone out for drinks and dinner with Christina's niece, Calliope, an island friend of many years and often her partner in teenage adventures with island boys. Now she stopped her rambling thinking and looked at the waiter she had continued her evening with after bidding Calliope goodnight.

He was, with his long wavy black hair, perfect lips and black eyes, a Greek god. Or Turkish, perhaps. She was not stupid, her teenage years long gone. He was, she guessed, a drifter, rootless, but that made him more interesting, not less. *The old-fashioned way*, she thought, *okay...* But before she could form her next thought, Patriki was standing in front of her, his arms around her waist; then kissing her, arching his crotch into hers as he did, his hand under her skirt, which, with one motion he pulled straight down. Then, still kissing her, he used both hands to pull her panties down as well. Her skirt and panties draped around her ankles, he pushed her against Christina's large butcher block table, went to his knees, spread her legs apart, and kissed and licked the inside of the thighs, and then her vagina, which was flowing with wetness. She arched her back against the edge of the table, pushing her clitoris against his darting tongue, delirious now, the Retsina adding fuel to her fire, in heaven.

No, she said, when he stopped licking, *don't stop...* But her new friend was now on his feet, swiveling her around, undoing his jeans and entering her from behind, his large hands hard on her buttocks. Wetter than ever, she felt herself convulsing from the rush of his first thrust, wanting more, wondering why he had stopped—again. *Don't stop.* She was about to turn to face him, when he grabbed her hair and twisted her head around so that they were looking into each other's eyes. His eyes were no longer liquid or playful; there was a coldness in them, a meanness. She tried to turn away, but he pulled harder on her hair to keep her facing him. So hard it hurt. Then he thrust again, and again, and the pain was gone and she was swept away in a swift current of pleasure.

14.

Brighton Beach, Brooklyn, August 24, 2012, 2:00 a.m.

I have gone out to get food and will
be right back. The door is open.

xxxooo
Natalya

Matt read the note in the dim light of Natalya's hall-way and let himself in. When he got back to his apartment after talking to Diego, one of the messages on his cell phone was from the singer at Sabrina's. "I must do a special show tonight, Matvey, at midnight. But it's my only show. Come to my apartment at two. We will talk and dance, and...and watch the sunrise. But no pictures! And no Nico to distract us."

Now he took a moment to glance around. The apartment's living room and small kitchen were divided by a waist-high counter, on which sat a bottle of unlabeled vodka, two shot glasses, two fluted glasses and a bottle of champagne in a bucket of ice. A Supremes song, *Baby Love*, was playing softly on a boombox on top of the refrigerator. Matt went over to see if he could find different music. Dialing slowly, humming *Baby Love* despite himself, he noticed the bill of a baseball cap sticking out from behind the boombox. He pulled it out, turned it to face him, and saw the logo on the front: a crowned soccer ball in yellow and blue with the letters *YKPAIHA* across it.

Matt turned the boombox off and listened. He could hear an air conditioner humming in the bedroom, which, up until a moment ago, he thought would be his final destination tonight. There was no air conditioner in the living room/kitchen. Through the open windows he could smell and hear the ocean just a few hundred feet away. On his own kitchen counter on Carmine Street was the lightweight Glock 17 nine-millimeter pistol that a person named Max had left in a tightly taped, nondescript cardboard box at his apartment door, along with a box of extra clips and ammunition. This was the same model plastic, easy trigger, no-kick Glock that his father and he had shot at a firing range in Jersey once a week for the four years he was in high school and living with his dad in SoHo. He had laughed when he read Max's note, but now wished he had the gun.

Out to get food, Matt thought, *with a huge restaurant kitchen downstairs, owned by her cousin.* The knock on the door did not startle him. He slipped the baseball cap back behind the boombox, then went over to the counter dividing the kitchen and living room and picked up the vodka bottle by its skinny neck.

"Natalya?" he said, flattening himself against the wall on the hinged side of the apartment's entrance door. His voice was normal, casual, happy to have his new lover home at last.

15.

Brighton Beach, Brooklyn, August 24, 2012, 2:15 a.m.

Max French did not mind waiting for people and things to come to him. He had been doing it on and off since he killed a certain someone in Auburn, Washington in 1982 when he was eighteen. He had the feeling, though, that tonight's wait would not be long, and he was right. A few minutes after crouching in the shadows at the back of the street-level entrance foyer to the apartment above Sabrina's and screwing the silencer onto his Sig P938 pistol, the door swung open and two men in ski masks stepped inside. Max stepped out and shot them both, once in the chest and once in the forehead each. He pulled their masks off and saw that they were no one he recognized, just young men, in their mid-twenties, with classic Slavic features. Hungarian, he guessed. Magyars. Disposable pawns. Before replacing the masks, he took a picture of each with his cell phone.

Then he went upstairs to get Matt.

16.

Skopelos, August 24, 2012, 6:00 p.m.

"I couldn't take a chance, Chris."

"I understand."

"I'm heading out to dump the bodies."

"Where's Matt?"

"In the kitchen. He almost killed me with a vodka bottle. I had to whack him."

"Is he okay?"

"He was groggy for a while but he's fine."

"Take him with you."

Silence. Then, from Max: "Are you sure?"

"Yes, it's started. There's no going back."

"Then what? "

"Call me tonight, 2:00 a.m. my time."

Chris Massi sat on the balcony of his library at the rear of his house on the western side of the island of Skopelos, looking down to the fifty hectares of olive grove laid out below him. The terraced hillside on which the grove stood was blanketed with the spiky yellow flowers—King's Spear his housekeeper, Christina, called them—that grew wild all over Greece. He had spectacular views of Panoramos Bay from the front of the house, but he liked to watch the sunset here because the sight of his thousand-year-old olive grove, with its gnarled branches and masses of gray-green leaves, settled his mind like nothing else he could look at or contemplate. A thousand years these trees had been standing here, thriving in winter cold and summer heat, oblivious of the joy and pain of the human beings who "owned" them, who harvested their fruit and pressed it into the dark green oil that had nourished them for generation after generation. Or were they? At night the leaves of his olive trees turned silver in the moonlight. When a breeze came up, they changed from silver to black, silver to black, and seemed to whisper to each other. Were they telling stories of man's folly? Trying to send Chris a message?

You did the right thing, Max. They were about to kidnap him, or worse.

Tess was here and safe. She would stay for another week, then fly back to New York. For his birthday she had brought him a CD of Sufi devotional music sung by a person named Nusrat Fatah Ali Khan. He could hear it playing now on the large terrace on the north side of the house. He listened closely for a moment to the singer's timeless, hypnotic voice, thinking of what Tess had said when she gave him the CD: you will think your olive trees are talking to you. Then he turned in the direction of the footsteps he heard on the tiled floor in the hallway that gave access to the library and the other rooms along this wing of the house.

"Come in Costa," he said in response to the two short hard raps on the library door. Costa's knock.

"Anadochos."

"Yes, Costa." Chris had risen from the cushioned rattan chair he was using on the balcony and went to sit at the scarred oak farm table he used as a desk just inside the room, his back to the open French doors behind him.

"The diamonds." Costa had quietly shut the study door and now stood before Chris, his gnarled hands steepled in front of him, his slight but very strong body motionless. Like one of my olive trees, Chris thought, not for the first time.

"Yes. What about them?" he said.

"A young woman was found dead in her apartment last month in Moscow. She worked for Alrosa."

"Russia's diamond company."

"Yes."

"Did she steal some diamonds?"

"Twenty-five mid-sized stones went missing in 2009. They were part of a delivery from Angola. She was a sorter. She was suspected as well as several others. The stones were never found and they never appeared on the black market."

"Go on."

"The woman's name was Irina Tabak. The police are looking for her boyfriend, a man named Andrei Kamarov. Here is his picture." Costa Vasiliou handed Chris an eight-by-ten piece of white copy paper, in the center of which was a black-and-white four-inch by four-inch image of a young man with short, light-colored hair and light eyes, probably blue. His pronounced Slavic features were set in near perfect symmetry in a square, open, handsome face. An innocent face.

Chris took the picture and studied it, but said nothing.

"They have been watching Irina for three years," Costa continued.

"And now she's dead," Chris said.

"Yes."

"And some diamonds appear for sale."

"Yes."

"Sit, Costa."

"No, Nonos, I will stand."

Chris had given up trying to get *Eleftheria's* captain to stop calling him godfather, or a diminutive of the word. Neither could he get his friend and employee of five years to relax when they were talking business. He looked at Costa now, taking in his nut brown, weather-beaten face, his expressionless liquid brown eyes, his hands still clasped, held at his waist. *Chtapodi* was the name he had given Vasiliou. The octopus. His tentacles were everywhere.

"There is more, Nonos," Costa said.

"Yes."

"Irina Tabak was Chechen. The police in Moscow think there is a connection to Caucasus Emirate."

"Mr. Umarov."

"Yes."

"You must thank your friends at Eleni's for me, Costa. In the usual way."

"I will, Nonos...Nonos?"

"Yes."

"We have company. A yacht in the bay."

"Someone new?"

"Yes."

"Probably rich Americans. But give me some pictures."

"Yes, Nonos."

Chris eyed Costa, remembering when they first met, in a police station in Athens in 2005. Who had saved whose life that night, exactly?

"Costa, you are my brother," he said, finally. "I am not your godfather." One more try.

"My life is yours, adelfos."

"I may need divers."

"How soon?"

"Tonight."

"Ochi problima."

"Where is Tess?"

"Sunbathing, I believe, with her new friend."

"The waiter?"

"Yes."

"Send someone to ask her to come up."

"Yes, Nonos."

As Costa turned to leave, there was a knock at the door. "Antikleidi," a woman's voice said.

"Come in Christina."

Chris's housekeeper, dark and handsome at age sixty, her jet-black hair streaked with gray at the temples, entered and quietly shut the door behind her. She had a cell phone in her hand. Chris studied her face as she silently handed him the phone. *Nothing*, he thought, *good*. On the phone's front screen was a telephone number in Cyrillic. The phone he was holding was Christina's, one he knew she used for everyday calls to the local markets, family and friends. Chris touched the speaker button and laid the phone on his desk. "Yes," he said.

"Mr. Massi?"

"Yes."

"Your daughter has paid us a visit."

Chris did not reply.

"If you step to one of your front rooms, you will be able see her on deck. You can't miss my yacht in the harbor. *Frie Markit*, it's called. You will need your binoculars."

"Who are you?" Chris said. He had not risen or moved anything except his full southern Italian lips as he spoke.

"I am a businessman. A Russian businessman."

"What do you want?"

"I would like to discuss a matter of international import with you. I am authorized to speak for the Kremlin in this matter. They have asked me for a favor."

Costa had stepped to a nearby cabinet, extracted a pair of Zeiss binoculars and left the room. Across the hall was a guest bedroom with a view of Panoramos Bay and its small, sheltered harbor. Through the open doors Chris watched as Costa raised the binoculars to his eyes, lowered them, and then turned to Chris and nodded.

"Let my daughter go, and we'll talk."

"Mr. Massi, your daughter is here of her own free will. It is just a fortunate coincidence that she paid us a visit. If you are watching you will see we are lowering the launch."

Costa put the binoculars to his eyes again, watched in complete stillness for thirty seconds, and then turned and again nodded to Chris.

"What's your name?"

"I am Marko Dravic."

"Mr. Dravic."

"Yes?"

"Come to my house for dinner tonight. We'll talk. Eight o'clock."

"Excellent. I will be there."

Chris pushed the red *end* bar on the phone.

"Do you still want the divers?" Costa asked. He was back in the study.

Christina was standing by the door. She had said nothing, but her eyes were burning. Tess had been coming to Skopelos twice a year since Chris bought the house and the restaurant on the beach below five years ago. "You are giving him dinner?" she blurted out now, before Chris could answer Costa's question.

"Yes, Christina," Chris replied, smiling, "and a good one, please." Then turning to Costa, he said, "Yes, Costa. Just one, tonight. Also, Costa, get me pictures of the launch when it drops Tess off at the dock."

17.

Jackson, New Jersey, August 25, 2012, 2:00 a.m.

Matt, covered by a sheen of sweat from hairline to toes, lay on his back on the faux leather couch in Wall Storage's office/waiting room, his hands clasped behind his head, looking up at the ceiling fan turning slowly above him. The two sheets he had used as bedding lay in a damp, sticky mass at his feet. He reached for the wet washcloth that Anna had given him in a bowl of ice and wiped the sweat from his neck and arms and chest. He did it slowly, saving his face for last. The ice cubes had melted, but the fan, though now working, was old and slow, and the tepid water against his hot skin was his only defense against the heat and humidity that had been pressing down on the Jersey shore for over a week, turning Anna's waiting room into a small, breathless cave. That and his youth and his memory of sleeping in the hold of the Scorpion as it trudged through similar nights on a windless Mediterranean. At least there was no smell of sour crude or engine oil to contend with here.

Earlier, having dinner on the concrete patio behind her living quarters, he and Anna had watched a full moon rise in a clear night sky. The last thing he saw before falling asleep were the stripes the Venetian blinds on the window behind him made on the far wall. Now they were gone and the room was full dark. Outside he could hear the wind whipping through the pine forest that surrounded Anna's small complex of buildings. A storm, he thought, to break this crazy weather.

On the floor under the couch was the Glock his new friend Max French had given him. Sitting up, he reached for the gun, checked that the safety was on, then slipped into his sandals. His black T-shirt, with *Isola Di Giglio* emblazoned in white script across the front, was on the coffee table next to him, but he left it there. It was still very hot and humid in the room. In cargo shorts and sandals, the Glock tucked into his belt, he padded to the front door to check that it was locked, then headed down the narrow hallway that lead to the rear door. He slid the bolt lock open and went into the concrete-floored room that contained Wall Storage's small lockers, in one of which, number 114, was Joseph Massi, Sr.'s two million in cash. The door that went to the small parking area in back was also locked. Bolted tight.

"They want the two million, but they also want you, Matt," Max French had said.

"Why?"

"To trade. That's my guess. They want something from your father."

"What?"

"I don't know."

"What about the diamonds?"

"They don't have to sell you the diamonds if they can just take the two million."

"Who are they?"

"We're not sure."

This conversation had taken place while Matt and Max were standing on the edge of an oily pond in the New Jersey Meadowlands surrounded by rushes and reeds that grew over their heads. At the bottom of this pond were the bodies of the two ski-masked men, weighted down with cinder blocks they had found strewn around the nearby mudflats, now bone dry after twenty days of ninety-degree weather and no rain. Remembering that scene, Matt said to himself, as he had many times in the last few days: *Grandpa Joe, what were you thinking?*

Matt did not have many memories of his paternal grandfather—known to a very small group of people as Joe Black Massi, the Mafia assassin—but the ones he had were vivid. The way the old man looked at him sometimes, as if he wanted to tell him a million things, but could say nothing, nothing that would make a difference. That look of sadness and love and something else, something that Matt was just now beginning to understand: *you will be tested,* Joe Black was silently saying, *and I will not be there to help.*

When he got back to the office Anna was standing in the middle of the waiting area in a scooped-neck T-shirt that reached to her thighs, pointing her Baby Glock at his head.

"It's me," he said. "I couldn't sleep."

"Kurva."

"What?"

"Fuck."

Outside, thunder cracked and rain started falling heavily. Some of it began splashing through the window behind the sofa, which was wide open. Anna ran to it and, kneeling on the couch, pulled it down, accentuating, as she did, a rounded, plump rear end beneath the light cotton of her shirt. She was still holding the Glock. When she turned back to face Matt, she put the gun on the coffee table, next to the *People* magazines. Matt put his Glock there as well. They stood for a moment, in the middle of the dark, overheated room, and looked at the two guns and then each other and listened to the rain coming down in sheets and the thunder now rolling in the distance. Matt, whose eyes had adjusted to the dark, could see the outline of Anna's breasts, the nipples pointing at him like the Glock had been a moment ago. His heart beating rapidly, he felt himself getting hard, uncontrollably, like when he was thirteen, and then *being* hard, very hard, his penis and heart throbbing with lives independent of his.

With his right foot, Matt slid the flimsy coffee table aside and stepped to Anna. When he reached her, he cupped her face in his hands and looked at her. Her mouth was shut tight, but she did not pull away. Who *was* she? Who was the person hiding behind that bad eye, that dark green thing adrift on its own that looked through him and away from him at the same time? His heart aching, and his loins, he kissed her, gently at first, feathering her lips apart with his tongue, then hungrily, pulling her against him, feeling with a shock her breasts through her thin shirt against his bare chest, the bulge of her belly against his penis. Still kissing her, feeding on her lips and teeth and tongue, he pressed her back toward the couch. She pulled away, startling him, but it was only to slip out of her shirt and panties, a second's work. On the couch she lay under him, her long legs wrapped around his back, as he entered her, shocked again at the sudden rush of pleasure as his mind and body—his entire being—became his penis for the five slow minutes it took him to climax. She moaned at the end too and, looking at her, he saw her eyes rolling upward, their spacing normal for an instant, and then the lids fall. He thought for a second she had fallen asleep, or even passed out, but then the lids, which he noticed for the first time were thickly lashed and blonde, lifted.

"Teo," Anna said, smiling languidly. "You are not gay like your gay uncle." For an answer, Matt laid his face between Anna's breasts and, breathing in her scent, listened to her heartbeat. "Christ," he whispered, "that was unbelievable."

Then, cocking his head slightly, Matt rose up and put his right index finger against Anna's lips, perpendicular to them. He lifted himself off of her and reached for his shorts on the floor near his feet. "Get dressed," he whispered, as he was stepping into them. "Take your gun. Go behind the counter."

"What...?"

"Do it."

While Anna was putting on her panties and T-shirt, Matt slid the safety off on his Glock, stepped over to the hallway that lead to the rear door, and listened. Nothing. What had he heard? A thump? A second hallway ran perpendicular to the back hallway, this one leading to Anna's bedroom, the first door on the left, and the kids's bedroom beyond that. Matt, walking slowly, could see that Anna's door was open. The Glock to his right ear, he looked in. Nothing. Then he heard another sound and saw the knob on the kids's door turning. He stepped over to the wall beside it and watched. The last time he had been in a situation like this he had swung a vodka bottle at Max French, who had deflected it with a sudden movement of his left arm, somehow managing to flip Matt to the floor and sit on him at the same time.

The kid's bedroom door swung in and Matt, still pressed to the wall, could sense that someone was standing there in the dark, looking into the hallway. Without thinking, he stepped in front of the person and lunged at his chest, using his head as a battering ram, driving the intruder deep into the room and crashing him against the far wall. They both went down, but

Matt jumped quickly to his feet, and pointed the Glock at his adversary's chest. "Stay there," he said. But the person either didn't see the gun or didn't care, because the next thing Matt knew there was a sharp pain in his right knee, and the intruder was on his feet, reaching behind his back for something. Matt stepped back and fired a round into his attacker's right leg, the one that had delivered the savage, lightning-quick kick to his knee. The intruder went down on his side, grabbing his leg. His gun had fallen to the floor with a thud. Matt picked it up and then, using his good leg, kicked him over onto his back. It wasn't a man. It was Natalya, her hair in a ponytail. Matt put the Glock to her forehead. "Stay there," he said. "Don't move."

He began to search her for more weapons, but did not get far when another person came jumping through the open bedroom window. Max French.

"Where were you?" Matt said.

"Sal fell off the roof. He broke his leg. He's with Nico."

"Who's this, Teo?" said Anna Cavanagh. She was standing in the doorway, pointing her Baby Glock at Max.

"He's a friend," Matt answered. "Can you get some rope?"

"She doesn't need rope," Anna said. "She needs a hospital." She had entered the room and was looking down at Natalya, whose eyes were wide open with hatred in the middle of a face now white, completely drained of color. "Fuck you," she mouthed to Anna.

"She's not going to a hospital," Max French said. "But a rope is a good idea. We'll tourniquet her leg. We don't want her to die just yet."

18.

Skopelos, August 25, 2012, 9:00 a.m.

"Did you sleep okay?"

"Yes. Are you angry?"

"Of course not."

"Who is he?"

"Who? Your waiter, or Dravic?"

"Well... both."

Chris and Tess were sitting on the north terrace, sipping coffee. A silver serving tray holding a loaf of the crusty bread Christina called *psomi kristina,* with a painted china plate of fresh butter next to it, rested on a small wrought iron table between them. From here they could see the whitewashed houses of the village arrayed in crooked rows on the hill that flanked

Panoramos Bay, which gleamed a hot blue-green under the Aegean's relentless morning sun.

"Tell me what happened?"

"I thought you'd never ask."

Chris smiled. Last night at dinner he had acted as if all was normal. Poised, very beautiful after two days in the sun, Tess, taking his cue, had lent a deft hand with the small talk over which the three courses of Christina's rich, deceptively simple meal were consumed. She had excused herself after the *baklava*, leaving him and Dravic to take their coffee and talk in the large, formal sitting room at the front of the house. Just another day in paradise.

"You handled yourself well," he said.

"What's going on, Dad?"

"What happened out there?"

"Patriki said he knew the chef on the new yacht in the harbor," Tess replied. "The owner was supposed to be away. He said his friend invited us for a drink and snack."

"How did you get there?"

"Patriki had his cousin's skiff. It took five minutes."

"What happened when you got there?"

"The owner *was* on board. Mr. Dravic. The chef was embarrassed. He had forgotten that he invited us."

"Did you believe him?"

"At the time I did."

"Then what?"

"Dravic was gracious. We sat on the bow deck and had lemonade and petit fours."

"Did you know he called me?"

"No."

"Then what?"

"He sent me ashore in the launch."

"And Patriki?"

"He said he wanted to stay and talk to his friend."

"He won't be back."

Chris watched his beloved Tess lower her eyes as he said this, and then raise them and look out over the village to the bay. The *Frie Markit* was gone.

"I'm sorry, Dad."

Chris Massi looked at his daughter, his first-born. At twenty-four, though he knew she would disagree and call herself a woman, she was still a girl. Beautiful, intelligent and proud, but still a girl. He did not want that to change any sooner than necessary, but the time had come.

"He has no cousin on the island," Chris said, "with or without a skiff. No family here."

"Who was he?"

"Someone who got paid to do a job, to demonstrate to me how easy it would be to abduct my daughter."

"How did Dravic get your cell number?"

"He called Christina's phone."

"How would he have that number?"

"He must have scanned it from your phone. There are devices that can do that." *Dravic's second mistake,* Chris thought.

"What did he want?"

"To mislead me in some way, I'm sure."

"About what?"

Chris did not answer. He looked out at the bay and then to his right, where he heard footsteps on the tiled terrace. Christina approached with a cell phone, which she handed to Chris.

"Mr. Max," she said.

"Max," Chris said, after taking the phone from Christina and putting it to his ear.

"It worked," Max said. "We have Nico and his partner."

"Andrei, you mean."

"Yes."

"Are they talking?"

"Not yet, but I haven't really tried. What should I do?"

"Start with the girl. Then confirm with Andrei."

"You know we're at the bottom of the food chain here."

"Get me to the top, Max."

"How much time do we have?"

"A couple of days."

"There's a complication."

"What?"

"The girl's hurt. Matt shot her in the leg. Also, Sal broke his leg jumping on Pugach. I'm sorry, *Kamarov*."

"Did you get her a doctor?"

"He's on his way."

"Max, someone made a play on Tess yesterday."

"What? Is she okay?"

"Yes, it was a warning."

"Connected to the diamonds?"

"I don't know. Yet."

"I'm on it."

"Thank you, Christina," Chris said, handing the phone to Christina after clicking off. "Are you still upset with me?" he asked her. He had to shade his eyes with his hand to be able to see her against the glare of the morning sun. "The dinner was good."

"Not so good," Christina replied. Then she turned and spat on the terrace and walked off. She probably spat in Dravic's food, Chris thought, watching her walk away.

Chris turned to Tess, who he knew from watching out of the corner of his eye had been listening intently to his side of his conversation with Max French.

"Who's Max?" she asked now.

"I want you to do me a favor, Tess," Chris said.

"What, Dad?"

"I want you to take some time off from graduate school."

"And do what?"

"I want you to go to a special school."

"What kind of school?"

"Weapons training, hand-to-hand, survival training, awareness training. Other stuff. It's geared toward women."

Chris watched his daughter's eyes as she reacted to this. No surprise, which was pretty surprising. What then? Enlightenment? Confirmation? Did she know something like this was coming? Maybe she *wasn't* a girl anymore. Maybe he'd misjudged her.

"How long?" she said.

"It's a one year commitment."

"Dad..."

"Yes."

"I don't have a choice, do I?"

"Not after last night, no."

"Where is it, the school?"

"In the desert in Arizona. And then Europe."

"When does it start?"

"A couple of weeks. Until then I want you to stay here. Costa's people will keep an eye on you."

"Can I date?"

"Tess."

"I'm kidding, Dad."

"Good."

"I have a picture of Patriki, if that means anything, on my phone."

"Send it to me, you never know."

"I will. Dad, I'll go to Arizona if you tell me what you really do."

"I run some businesses that your grandfather passed on to me, that's all."

"Dad..."

"You have to go, Tess."

19.

Jackson, New Jersey, August 25, 2012, 5:00 a.m.

Matt and Anna sat on folding beach chairs on the concrete slab that served as a front porch for Wall Storage. The rain had stopped, leaving the small asphalt parking lot glistening under the twin pole lamps that straddled the front gate and the night air cool and smelling of pinesap and ozone. Anna, dressed in jeans, sandals and a dark blue polo shirt had made a pot of coffee, which sat, with their cups and spoons and a sugar bowl, on a white plastic table between them. They had a good view of the front gate and the long, quiet road that led to it through the forest of scrub pine from Route 195, a major highway about ten miles away. Matt, watching the road, fingered his bruised right knee, which had been iced and bandaged by the same Air Force doctor who had set Sal Visco's broken ankle and tended to what had turned out to be a flesh wound in Natalya's leg. He looked at his watch. The flight from McGuire to Warsaw was scheduled to leave at 6:00 a.m. He had told Max he would be back in time but he doubted he would. To make the plane, he would have to leave now, which he would not do.

"Are you sure he's coming?" Matt asked.

"No."

"What did he say?"

"He said that he had enough. He was coming over."

"Does he know where your friend lives?"

"He thinks they are here with me, the kids."

"Does he own a gun?"

"Not that I know of."

Anna had brought a pack of Marlboro Lights out with her on the coffee tray. She tapped one out now, lit it with a plastic lighter, inhaled deeply, tilted her head back and blew a long slow stream of smoke out into the air above her.

"What happened tonight?" she asked, when she was done.

"They wanted the cash."

"Yes, but the other man, Max. Who is he?"

"I just met Max. Sal, you know."

"You are not answering."

"Max is a new friend. Please don't ask me anything else about him."

"What happened?"

"Max and Sal were waiting for them on the roof."

"Why?"

"Max wanted to talk to them."

"Why?"

"I'm not sure, Anna, I'm really not."

"Did you know they were up there? On the roof?"

"I knew they'd be in the area, that's all."

"Where did you go?"

"I can't tell you."

"Why are you here?"

Why *am* I here? Matt thought. Then he looked over at Anna, picked her beautiful face out of the gray, pre-dawn light, and remembered their lovemaking, the smell and feel of her unbelievable body, her moaning beneath him, his sudden, convulsive climax. It made him dizzy, this memory. *That* was the reason, that memory, for the rush he felt when she called him on his cell. It all came back to him when he heard her voice. He could no more say no to her than he could stop himself from breathing. *That's why you're here, Matt.*

"Because you asked me to come," he replied, finally.

"And you came."

"Yes."

"Like *that*," she said.

"Yes."

"It's just the sex," she said.

"Maybe. But what's wrong with that?"

"Nothing."

"Tell me about Skip," Matt said. "How did he try to kill you?"

"With a baseball bat he keeps in his truck." Anna stood and lifted her blouse, revealing the lurid remains of her twelve-inch by twelve inch, Rorschach test of a black and blue mark.

Matt looked.

"He was going to hit me again," Anna said, "but he was drunk. He swung at my head, slipped on one of my son's toys and hit his head on the corner of the kitchen counter. I had already called 911. The police arrived and took him away."

"Was this the first time?"

"A year ago," Anna answered, and then stopped, as if this were all she was going to say, her mouth grim. Then she went on: "He tried to run me over with his truck. I ran. He hit the fence. He had started drinking again. He was also using the meth. A friend of his makes it. Crystal meth, the cops called it, such a nice name for such a bad thing."

Before he could respond, Matt heard the sound of a car and, looking up, saw headlights approaching the gate. As they drew nearer and stopped, he saw it was a red pickup, its fenders and sides streaked with mud.

"I guess this is him," Matt said, eying the driver, who was stabbing with his index finger at the keypad mounted on a post at the entrance. Matt got to his feet as did Anna.

"If he is drunk," Anna said, "he will be nasty."

Matt watched Skip Cavanagh park his truck in a space near the front gate, exit and walk over to them. He was bigger than Matt had expected, six-three, a couple hundred pounds, cut, a weightlifter, tattoos on both of his forearms. His hair was long, well below his

ears, and straggly, his square face darkened by a two-
or three-days growth of beard. As he came closer Matt
could see the sneer on his face and the meanness in his
eyes.

"Who are you?" Cavanagh asked when he reached
the porch.

"I'm Anna's friend," Matt replied. "Matt Massi."

"Matt Massi. Am I supposed to be impressed? Who
the fuck are you?"

"I told you, I'm Anna's friend."

"You are not allowed to be here," Anna said. "You
are drunk."

"I want to see the kids."

"You can't."

"Oh no?" Cavanagh turned as if to walk away, then
turned back with a pistol in his hand, which he pointed
at Anna and then Matt. "Go get the kids, Anna, or your
new boyfriend's a dead man."

"Wait," Matt said, "let's talk. Here, have some coffee."
As he said this, Matt reached for the glass coffee pot,
held it up to his chest as if it were a chalice filled with
wine, or nectar, a peace offering, and then, using both
hands, flew it at Cavanagh's face. Anna's husband, his
eyes widening, stepped back to avoid the coffee pot, but
not quickly enough. The pot thumped against his forehead, spilling hot coffee onto his face and chest. It broke
into pieces with a sharp *crack* when it hit the ground.
Matt pulled his Glock from his belt and stepped toward Cavanagh who, reeling backward, aimed his gun
at Matt. Then Matt heard a shot and Cavanagh went

down, his gun clattering to the ground. Turning quickly, Matt saw Anna holding her Glock out in front of her.

"I thought you never used it?" he said, turning back just as quickly to face the man on the ground.

"He was going to kill you," Anna replied, moving to stand next to Matt. "And then me."

They watched as Cavanagh, bleeding from his right thigh, grunted, sat up and began groping for his gun, which was at his feet. Matt stepped forward and kicked the gun away in one swift movement, then fired a round directly into Cavanagh's heart.

About to die, Skip Cavanagh stared at Matt for one mad second and then fell backward, blood oozing from his wounds, his arms splayed in supplication.

Matt pulled out his cell phone and dialed a number.

"Uncle Frank," he said when his call was answered. "I have a problem."

20.

Skopelos, August 25, 2012, 10:00 a.m.

Chris shaded his eyes and looked out at the harbor. *Eleftheria* had moved during the night to an anchorage just inside the rocky spit of land that formed the southern pincer of Panaramos Bay. Sheltered as she was, she could still be at sea in under five minutes. He took his cell phone from the front pocket of his white linen shirt and tapped a speed dial screen.

"Anadochos," Costa Vasiliou said.

"Costa, the picture you showed me, Andrei Kamarov."

"Yes."

"He also goes by Nico Pugach. He worked on the Scorpion with Matt."

"Yes, Anadochos."

"I need to know who he is. His family, everything."

"It will be done."

"And Mr. Dravic, the same."

"Ochi problima, Nonos."

"And our waiter friend? Was I right?"

"Yes, Nonos. A drifter."

"Any friends?"

Silence.

"Just Tess."

"Yes, Nonos. He was hired to do a job."

"Has he returned?"

"He will not return. His body will be dumped at sea."

"I agree. Thank you, Costa."

Chris powered his phone down and put it back in his shirt pocket. He had woken up thinking of his conversation with Marko Dravic over coffee last night. Now he went over it again in his mind:

What does the Kremlin want of me, Mr. Dravic? I am just a businessman.

They want you to help stop a terrorist attack.

Who are they?

GRU. I assume you know who they are.

No, tell me.

It is Russia's military foreign intelligence agency. Its civilian counterpart is SVR.

What do they think I can do that they can't do themselves?

The attack will take place in Prague. GRU has certain information that could help prevent it. You have business interests in Prague. You will be the intermediary between GRU and SIS. Do you know SIS?

It must be the Czech domestic intelligence agency.

Yes, correct.

Why do they need an intermediary?

They hate us in Prague. They will not believe us.

If it works out, you could mend fences.

They hate us. You know why of course.

You had your boot on their throat for fifty years. Two generations.

I see you are an idealist, Mr. Massi. A rarity in your line of work.

Chris had let this pass.

Are you interested?

Does U.S. intelligence know about this?

They do not believe it to be credible.

Who have you spoken to?

Ah, that is a murky world, Mr. Massi. I have spoken to no one. But others have.

Who's behind the attack?

GRU believes Caucasus Emirate. Do you know them? Chechen Islamists?

There are lots of groups that I hear about.

Yes, I'm sure.

How do I reach you?

Here is a number to call. Just leave a message. "Prague Yes." Simple.

It won't be me who leaves the message.

I understand.

And if I say yes?

Ah yes, the payoff.

Chris had remained silent. They were in a sitting room next to the north terrace, facing each other in the linen-covered minimalist lounge chairs that had been a housewarming gift to Chris from a client in Morocco. An intermittent breeze coming in through the room's open windows and French doors cooled them and occasionally brightened the flames of the simple black candles that Christina had lit on the small marble table between them when she brought the coffee. In the candle glow Dravic's pale face had been pleasant enough, his blue eyes not without warmth, but rarely was anyone cast to type in Chris's world, where villains could and often did look like angels and angels like circus freaks.

Until now Chris had kept his distance, suggesting by the quietness of his gaze and the stillness of his body the temperament simply of a cautious businessman listening to a proposal, an exotic proposal, but just a business proposal, nevertheless. Now he looked carefully at the fifty-something, clear-eyed, sandy-haired Russian sitting across from him sipping Christina's coffee from the house's best espresso cups, his manners and his English impeccable.

Let us say, Dravic had finally said, you will be left alone.

21.

Panaramos Bay, Skopelos, August 27, 2012, 10:00 p.m.

"Have you spoken to Matt?" Max French asked.

"Yes. He's coming here tomorrow."

"What happened?"

"The woman at the storage place."

"I thought so," Max replied, remembering the image of Anna Cavanagh in her low-necked T-shirt, gun in hand, yellow hair falling randomly to her shoulders, like something from the soldier of fortune magazines he read when he was a boy. He loved those fucking magazines. And then there was that bad eye. How sexy was that?

"What did he tell you?" Chris asked.

"He told me he had something to do, that he'd be back for the flight. Sal couldn't go with him. He never came back."

"The woman. You met her. Who is she?"

"She's a Czech national," Max replied, "who married an American. Two young kids. One eye is cocked. She's tall and blonde, thirtyish."

Max paused to gauge Chris's reaction. He was waiting for more.

"Yes, she's good-looking," he said.

"What else?"

"I only saw her for a few minutes."

"Nothing?"

Max paused again. This is why I like working for this guy, he thought, he knows me for the freak I am.

"She has a secret," Max said, finally.

"Good. Find out what it is."

"I will."

Max French had met Chris Massi in 2004 and, though he had worked with him three times since, this was only the second time he had been face-to-face with him. He eyed him now across *Eleftheria's* mutely lit below-decks lounge, trying, with little success, to assess the changes in the man whose father had been a professional killer and who had himself gotten away with murder in 2003. When Massi did not reply after a long thirty seconds, Max decided to speak.

"These things happen, Chris," he said. "He's twenty-two."

"I understand."

"I'm the only one they trust in Warsaw," Max said. "You said we only had a few days."

"You had to leave."

"Yes." But I don't blame Matt for staying behind, for disobeying his father. I might have too. For Ms. Cavanagh. That eye! It makes her more beautiful.

"What did you do in Warsaw?"

"Waterboard. It only took an hour."

"They were in sync?"

"Yes."

"Are they related?"

"Brother and sister."

"What did they have to say?"

"They believed they were working for the *Odessa Mafya*."

"Don Marchenko," Chris said. "*Odessa Bratva*."

"Yes. They were to do everything they could to sell the diamonds to Matt. When they found out about the two million, they killed the locksmith and went after the cash."

"Skip the diamonds. It makes sense."

"The thing is, they were acting on their own when they went after the cash. They got the storage unit number from a local locksmith and then killed him."

"You're kidding?"

"No. They were told if they couldn't make the deal with Matt, they were to come home. They never told their contact about the cash or the locksmith."

"The locksmith wasn't in on it?"

"No."

"Did he have a family?"

"Two kids."

"How did they know they were working for Odessa Bratva?"

"Their contact told them."

"Who was that?"

"The captain of the Scorpion."

"Stavros."

"Yes."

"So they had to sell these particular diamonds and it had to be to Matt."

"It looks that way."

"Did he talk about his so-called girlfriend, Irina Tabak?"

"He was paid to kill her."

"By whom?"

"A man he met in a bar in Odessa."

"Eliminated by now, I'm sure."

"I agree. What now? You haven't told me about Tess."

"A Russian named Marko Dravic got her out to his yacht on the bay."

"How?"

"He used a handsome drifter, a waiter in town. He said he knew the chef—that Dravic was away. They were supposed to have a drink. All in the open."

Max shook his head. He had never met Tess Massi, but had fallen in love with her picture, a phenomenon in his life that he knew was a problem that would one day have to be confronted. He fell in love with pictures, not real women. "Is she still here?" he asked.

"Yes."

"What did Dravic want?"

"He wants me to carry a message to SIS in Prague. GRU has come upon a plot to set off bombs in Wenceslas Square on September eleven."

"By whom?"

"The Chechans. Supposedly."

"Everything is *supposedly* until it happens in this business."

Chris nodded.

"Why you?"

"That's the big question," Chris replied. "He said the Czechs won't believe the Kremlin, too much bad blood."

"What do you think?"

"I think it might be about me."

"You? How?"

"An old grudge. A score to settle."

"They picked a pretty elaborate way to do it."

"I agree."

"What do you want me to do?"

"Costa is checking out Dravic. You do the same. Go to Prague. Talk to our people there. Ask them if they hear anything about an attack in Wenceslas Square on 9/11."

"Should I let Mr. White know what's going on?" Max asked.

"Yes. I may need his help. My children are involved."

"Should I tell him that?"

"Yes."

"What kind of help? In case he asks."

"Reconnaissance. Maybe a drone."

"A *drone*? Chris..."

"You know the deal we made, Max."

"Okay," Max said, thinking, *that's the problem when you have kids, people you love.* Then, out loud, he said, "Chris, about Matt..."

"He's on his own, Max. It was always going to come down to that. I'm responsible."

Max, who had gotten away with a murder of his own, when he was eighteen, and who was a keen if unorthodox observer of human nature, now knew that the reason he was having trouble seeing the changes Chris Massi had undergone was because they had been natural, a matter of evolution, that the judgment Mr. White had made in 2004 had been accurate. More than accurate—prescient. He was about to push out of his comfortable chair to take his leave when he was interrupted by Chris.

"Before you go, Max."

"Yes."

"How are you?"

Max brought himself to the edge of his chair and answered without thinking, "I'm fine." Then he thought, *he means it.*

"Do you know what we have in common, Max?" Chris asked.

"What?"

"An unconscious operating principal."

"What is it?"

"If I knew, it wouldn't be unconscious anymore."

"When you figure it out, let me know."

"I will," Chris replied, smiling. "Then we can both retire."

22.

Moscow, August 28, 2012, 7:00 a.m.

"So, Marko, what happened to your young man and his sister?"

"I don't know. I assume they are dead or being held somewhere very secure."

"No trace?"

"No."

"You have people looking, searching, inside and out?"

"Yes."

"What went wrong?"

"I don't know."

"Mr. Massi, Senior, may have intervened."

"Yes. I assume the son reported the offer to the father, which is what we wanted." *What you wanted*, Marko Dravic said to himself.

"You deliberately hired amateurs."

"Yes, with nothing to talk about if they got caught."

"Except the ship's captain, whom I assume you have taken care of."

"Yes, I have."

"Perhaps your young man talked about Ms. Tabak and her diamonds."

"That contact has also been eliminated."

"No man, no problem."

"Yes. Stalinesque."

"Oh, that's been going on for centuries. Look at Julius Caesar, Saddam Hussein. It's a boring list."

"They didn't die well."

"As I say, quite boring. And futile, really."

"I agree." *What else would I do, but agree with you?*

"We will save the diamonds for another day."

Marko Dravic, nee Marko Dravnova—and with many other aliases in between—sat across from the man known in a very small circle as the Wolf, the secret head of possibly the most secret espionage unit in the world. "How do you wish me to proceed?" he asked.

"Massi will go to Prague."

"Why, because his children have been put into play?"

"Yes, it is the typical response. You can always count on American sentimentalism."

Dravic, who had been wondering if he would be the Wolf's next meal—the operation in America had been a complete failure—did not agree. Massi had no country. He had a kingdom, a moveable kingdom. "And once in Prague?" he asked.

"He must meet with one of the Iranian madmen. Someone directly linked to Fallen Heroes. You will arrange that. Get a photograph if you can."

"They will want to know why, the Iranians and their Syrian friends."

"What shall we tell them?"

Dravic was in no hurry to respond. He had been buried deep in the Odessa underworld for many years, running a vast credit card theft operation, which included thief-to-thief escrow accounts and the manufacture and sale of ATM skimmers, with profits in the hundreds of millions, most of it going to the Wolf's numerous personal accounts and operational slush funds. He had killed several men personally in that time and ordered the deaths of a dozen others. Other than the money it raised for Mother Russia, he did not know nor did he care why the Wolf had put him in that job. The same went for his current assignment.

"That Massi is an American spy who we are trying to destroy?"

"No, they would want no part of that."

"Then what?"

"That Massi is *our* man, that there will be no deal for oil products, no cover at the UN, unless he is involved, unless we use his ships."

"*Is* he our man?"

"No."

"*Is* he an American spy?"

"I think he is."

There must be easier ways than this to eliminate him, Dravic thought. Then, out loud, he said, "So I am a fellow businessman, who can vouch for him and who has your imprimatur?"

"Excellent."

"And why should they produce someone from Fallen Heroes?"

"Because we insist, because Assad will fall without our oil products. Remind them how much tank fuel we are ready to supply. And because we can stop the Iranian nuclear program whenever we want."

"Shall I be that blunt?"

"If they resist, yes."

The two men, both 1975 graduates of the Soviet Union's 401st KGB school in Ochta, Leningrad, both sixty years-old, sat in a small but beautifully appointed office situated in the rotunda of the southeast corner tower of the Cathedral of Christ the Savior on the Moscow River. To the east they could see the towers of the Kremlin rising above the Alexander Gardens, and below them the traffic speeding along the Kremlin Embankment. The late-summer day promised to be warm and sunny, but the night had been cool, bracing in fact, presaging Russia's great historical guardian and true savior, winter. Old hands, Marko and his boss could smell winter in the air, along with danger—and opportunity.

"Do you find that chair comfortable?" the Wolf asked.

Dravic shifted his weight in the heavy-framed velvet-covered chair. "Yes," he answered.

"They were gifts, these chairs, from the bishop here, Father Josef."

"When you built this secret office."

"Yes. You don't know Father Josef, do you, Marko?"

"No, I don't think I do."

"He was a year behind us at Octha. They called him the Matador."

"The Matador?"

"He raised red flags wherever he went."

"And now he is a bishop."

"Yes, he was useless as a spy but he came from an important family, so Andropov made a deal with him. 'Enter the priesthood, we will guide you to the top, you will work for us as needed. If you refuse, you die or go to an asylum.' He was thinking ahead, Yuri, even then, you see."

"He was wrong about the space creatures."

Both men smiled. The head of the KGB for fifteen years before becoming General Secretary, Yuri Andropov had a keen interest in UFOs, certain that space aliens would one day become Russia's natural allies in the cold war. The thousands of monitoring stations he had had built across three continents and manned around the clock had all been abandoned when the Soviet empire broke up in 1990.

"Yes," the Wolf said, "but he foresaw the changes we now see in place, what the West calls the new world order. And he hedged our mother's bets."

"Our dear Mother Russia."

"Which brings us back to your present mission."

"I am listening."

"You will need help outside the normal channels."

"I agree."

"The Christians in Syria have not joined the uprising. You are aware of this?"

"Yes. Assad has left them alone."

"And his father before him."

"It seems we are their protectors."

"Quite right. And so for this and for many other things, the church is in our debt."

"So I have gathered. You are leading up to something."

Here the Wolf smiled broadly, showing a full set of good strong teeth, the canines just slightly larger than the rest on top. At Octha, he was the wolf with a lower case w. Now, having survived the breakup of the Soviet Union, the dismantling of the KGB and risen high in the GRU, the w, in Dravic's mind at least, was writ large.

"Do you watch television, Marko?"

"Rarely."

"Do you know the handsome young priest, Father Nicolei Petrov?"

"No."

"He is a star in the church and the media."

"The media?"

"Yes, he is often on television. He takes the tradiional side in all the debates, the church's side."

"As I said, I do not watch television."

"He is the darling of the religious right, not only here in Russia, but throughout Central Europe."

"Is he one of ours? Is that it?"

"His sister, Valentina," the Wolf replied, "is his secretary and manager. She books him on talk shows, parliamentary hearings, she travels with him for his appearances in foreign capitals."

"Is *she* one of ours?"

"Yes and no."

"The best answer."

"You are staying at the National, as usual," the Wolf asked.

"As usual."

"Valentina and Father Nicolei will be having dinner there tonight with friends. Be at the bar at ten p.m. She will walk through to the ladies room. She is thirty-five, five-seven in height, long dark hair, dark eyes. Very beautiful. She'll be wearing a black dress with a diamond necklace. She will leave instructions there for you in the soap dispenser, the name of your contact at the Iranian embassy in Prague and your contact code."

"The ladies room is lockable?"

"Yes."

"Cameras?"

"Operated with the light switch. Do not turn it on."

"Simple."

The Wolf smiled his toothy smile, the canines fully on display. "As we were taught," he said.

Yes, Marko Dravic thought, but we were also taught not to be obsessive, not to let it get personal. Sentiment kills Americans, not us. So why are you obsessed with Mr. Chris Massi when this operation would be so simple without him? Indeed, would there even be an Operation Fallen Heroes if you could not get Mr. Massi involved?

23.

Skopelos, August 28, 2012, 6:00 p.m.

Chris Massi's private beach was strung along the south side of a small, crescent-shaped cove that could hardly be noticed on a map as distinct from the larger expanse of the bay. Its sand was a strange sparkling lava-gray and its waters a pale, translucent green, a dreamy pastel canvas that did not darken until the ocean floor fell away a hundred yards out toward the horizon. Here Chris swam every afternoon when he was in Skopelos, swam and occasionally read, before showering and then checking the layout of his world, the moving and non-moving parts, the pieces he could control and those he could only watch. Today, turning toward shore, he saw his son and daughter on the beach, sitting on the wooden chairs Christina kept between two boulders at the foot of the cliff, at the summit of which stood his hundred-year-old rambling whitewashed house. He had caught a quick glimpse of them descending the stone steps that led down the steep cliff from the house as he was turning into his last lap. There would be no reading today. Today there would be questions.

Tess greeted him at the surf's edge with a thick over-sized towel. As he dried off he watched Matt—who had landed in Athens last night and on Skopelos that morning—pour white wine from a bottle that was on ice in a silver bucket on the sand. At breakfast, they had not pressed him for information and he had been pleased. *Think*, he had said to them as they were growing up, apropos of matters large and small. An argument with a coach? A teenage betrayal? An injustice to be confronted? Think before you speak or act. Slow down. *Do not be over-eager. Do not show your hand before it is absolutely necessary.* But he could read their faces. *Training in Arizona? Max French? Dead bodies in the New Jersey Meadowlands? McGuire Air Force Base? Warsaw?* They wanted to know about his world, of which he had told them nothing since the day he entered it eight years ago. He was not surprised to see them waiting for him.

"We thought we'd surprise you," Matt said, handing the wine glasses around.

"*Yassas*," Chris said, smiling, raising his glass.

"*Yassas*," echoed Tess and Matt.

Tess and Matt sat, and Chris, the setting sun to his back, sat facing them in the chair they had placed there for him. In a canvas bag on the sand was a black cotton sweater, which Chris pulled out and slipped on. The first sip of wine was tangy as it mixed with the residue of sea salt on his lips. The second was clean and bright and resiny, the bottle, he knew, coming from Christina's homemade store in the cellars beneath the house.

"Dad," Matt said, "Tess told me she's going to Arizona."

"And then Italy," Chris said.

"Italy?" Tess said.

"For the second part of your training."

"I think I should go too," said Matt.

"Not now," Chris answered.

"What's going on, Dad?" Matt asked.

"Let's back up," Chris said. "Tell me about Uncle Frank."

"Uncle Frank," Matt replied, his face grim. "Did you talk to him?"

"Yes."

"What did he say?"

"You had a problem. You called him. He took care of it."

"That's it?"

"There was a dead body. You and a woman were on the scene."

"What dead body?" Tess asked. "What woman?"

"It doesn't matter," Chris said, his eyes on Matt. "Tell me about her, the woman."

Matt did not answer. He looked at Tess for a long second or two and then back at Chris.

"Go ahead," said Chris.

"Her name is Anna Cavanagh, born Anna Cervenka," Matt said, and then stopped and looked at Chris. "Everything?" he said.

Chris nodded.

"Grandpa Joe left me two million dollars," Matt said, looking at his sister now, whose eyes, Chris saw, narrowed in concentration around an otherwise fully composed face. "I just found out about it. It's in a self-storage place at the shore. Anna owns the storage place. Nico—you met him, Tess—asked me if I wanted to buy some diamonds; he said I'd make a huge profit. He somehow found out about the two million. He tried to steal it. Also to kidnap me, I *think* kidnap me, I'm not sure."

Matt stopped and turned to Chris. "This is the crazy part," he said. "What happened, Dad?"

Chris looked at his son and his daughter and then up at the top of the cliff, where three men with AK-47s stood at fifty-foot intervals in silhouette against the evening sky. Surely Matt and Tess had noticed them. Costa's men, from the Café Eleni. He looked at his children again, one to the other. Who were they? What blood ran in their veins? No answers. Nevertheless, the time had come.

"When you told me about Nico and the diamonds, I sent my friend Max French to keep an eye on you," Chris said. "He intercepted your kidnappers and killed them. He figured Nico and his sister would try to steal the money again. He caught them and took them to

Poland to interrogate them. They believed they were working for a Russian Mafia boss."

Chris stopped to look at Matt and Tess, who seemed to him to be in a state of suspended animation, between two worlds, much as he was on the day in 1977 when he was sixteen and his father told him he killed people for a living. He didn't know then that it would come to this, but he should have. *Inevitability*, he thought, the last puzzle before death and God.

"Who were the kidnappers?" Tess asked.

"Probably friends of Nico's from Little Odessa," Chris replied. "Nico probably promised them part of the two million."

"I helped Max bury the bodies," Matt said, addressing Tess, who remained focused and poised, like a queen, Chris thought, listening to the report of a battle.

"Matt was supposed to go to Poland with Max," Chris continued, "but Anna Cavanagh called and asked him for help. Her drunken husband was threatening her. That's where Uncle Frank comes in. What happened, Matt?"

"The husband was very drunk, or high on speed. Or both. He pulled a gun. I had no choice."

"Then what?"

"I called Uncle Frank. An hour later, two guys in a pickup truck showed up," Matt replied. "They looked like farmers. They took the body away, and all the guns and the husband's truck."

"That's it?" Chris asked.

"They scrubbed the blood off the parking lot with some kind of solvent. I'm sorry, Dad."

"For what?"

"Uncle Frank. You're in his debt."

"That's not a problem," said Chris. "Trust me."

"Should I have called *you*?" Matt said.

"You can always call Uncle Frank," Chris replied. "He works for me."

Now both Massi siblings were silent.

"So," Tess said. "What's going on? Who's Max French? How come we never heard of him before?"

Chris looked at his daughter before answering. *Just like that,* he thought. *She's in.*

"He used to be in the FBI," Chris replied. "Now he works for himself, and for me."

"Poland?" Matt asked. "That's where we do our renditions, isn't it?"

"We have friends there," Chris replied.

"Wait," Tess said. "Are you talking about *you* personally or the United States government?"

"Both," said Chris. "And neither."

Chris was looking at Tess but out of the corner of his eye he saw a quick wry smile cross Matt's face.

"You said Nico *thinks* he was working for the Russian Mafia," Tess said. "Who was he really working for?"

"I don't know," Chris replied. "But I need to find out."

"Can we help?" Matt asked.

"You're in the thick of it, Matt," Chris answered. "That's why you're here."

"Is it Marko Dravic?" Tess asked.

"Who's Marko Dravic?" said Matt.

"Tess has a story of her own to tell," Chris said. "I'm going up to shower. Tell him, Tess. I'll see you at dinner."

∧ ∧ ∧ ∧ ∧

"You *killed* a guy?" Tess said when Chris was gone.

"Yes. But don't ask me about it."

"Okay, but what about Anna Cavanagh, *born Anna Cervenka*? Are you in love with her?"

Matt did not reply. 'Matt the Mute' had been one of Tess's nicknames for her brother when they were teenagers. When he wasn't swaggering his idiotic Mafia-princeling swagger he was as silent as marble, and as dense, unable to formulate a coherent thought.

"You have to be," she said. "You killed her husband to protect her."

"Why the sarcasm?" Matt asked.

"What sarcasm?"

"Born Anna Cervenka."

He loves her, Tess thought; he hates her married name. And there's something else I'm not getting. What? Does Matt have a secret?

"He killed himself," Matt said, without waiting for Tess to answer.

"You mean by pulling a gun on you?" she said.

"Yes."

All her life Tess had wondered what would become of Matt, the only grandson of a Mafia don on one side and a Mafia hit man on the other. Now he had killed someone. Made his bones as they used to say.

"What's she like, Anna Cervenka?" Tess said, shifting gears, hoping to get the thing out of her brother that she knew he was holding back. "Come on. I'm not teasing you. *Are* you in love with her?"

"I just met her."

"That doesn't mean anything."

"I don't know, Tess. I am and I'm not."

"You had great sex."

Silence.

"It's a game changer, great sex."

Matt's eyes darted at hers, but he remained silent.

"Where is she now?" Tess asked.

"She's in New York. I gave her some money. I also got someone to watch her place."

"Is the money still there? The two million?"

"No. I moved it."

"I don't think Dad's the head of the DiGiglio Mafia family," Tess said. "I should say, I think he's *that* and something else."

"Who's Marko Dravic?" asked Matt.

"Do you agree?" Tess asked.

Matt did not reply. The siblings looked at each other, their beautiful, sensuous faces and lithe bodies like pre-Raphaelite figures bathed in the slanting rays of the late-day Aegean sun.

"I agree," he said at length.

"He kidnapped me. Dravic."

"What? What happened?"

"I was drugged."

"What?'

"By great sex."

"What?"

Tess told Matt the story of her brief affair with the handsome young man who called himself Patriki Karros, of her abduction in broad daylight. She left out the intimate details but did not gloss over the key point: she had been drugged by great sex; she would have gone anywhere with Patriki.

"Yes, Matt," she said at the end. "Women like sex."

"I know they do."

"Your sister included."

"Tess..."

"The thing is, Matt, I was a fool, and I can't be from now on. And neither can you. Your friend Nico would have killed you for that money."

"And Marko Dravic, what did he want from Dad?"

"I don't know, Dad didn't tell me."

"Is he connected to Nico and the diamonds?"

"I think that's what Dad's trying to find out."

"*Renditions*, Tess? *Warsaw*? They waterboard in Warsaw. They do SERE."

"What's SERE?"

"Sensory overload. A form of torture."

"How do you know about this stuff?"

"I'm doing my senior thesis on it, that is, I am if I ever get back to New York."

"On torture?"

"No, on black ops."

"Christ..."

"It's what Dad does, Tess, face it."

24.

Ephesus, August 29, 2012, 8:00 a.m.

Though he knew the old man was a cold-blooded killer, some said a psychopath, Chris liked Viktor Marchenko almost instantly. Not because he was unpretentious or unassuming. The frayed white cotton shirt, the thick Turkish coffee—served in an old fashioned stove-top pot with a long wooden handle, by a middle-aged daughter who had lost whatever beauty she may have once had—were as likely an act, a *presentation*, as not. Nor was he gracious. He was a prickly old man, who it was obvious did not like to be bothered by extraneous details or to deal directly with anyone outside his inner circle. No, it was just that the white-haired don's light brown eyes were as keenly intelligent as any he'd seen. Only his ex-father-in-law's came close. They were dons of the old school, interested in the big picture and the future. How to fathom the one and arrive safely and intact in the other.

"How shall I address you," Marchenko said, "should I choose to?"

"I would be honored if you would call me Chris, or Christopher."

"You have very good friends," Marchenko said.

"Thank you. They honor me."

"I have never met Don DiGiglio. It was a pleasure to speak to him. Will you be seeing him when you leave here?"

"No."

"He says you are now the head of the family. We are equals, you and I, and thus I agreed to meet you."

Chris let this pass. They were sitting on heavy wooden chairs in a sunken garden on the old Russian's estate in Ephesus, on Turkey's Mediterranean coast. Their feet nearly touched the pebbled scree that bordered a small pond, on the smooth dark surface of which water lilies silently floated, their white faces turned to the sun. They were surrounded by a crumbling stone wall overgrown with thorny shrubs and vines. Beyond the wall dense brush encircled the garden and beyond that thickly wooded hills rose on all sides. On one hilltop Chris could see what was left of more ancient stonework, a battlement or a rampart last used a thousand years ago. He could hear the sea, which he knew from the reconnaissance photos that Max had provided him was only a hundred yards or so away to the south. No one else was about, though Chris had no doubt that the armed men who had escorted him to the grotto were not far away, were watching them in fact. On a stone slab next to Marchenko was a thick-handled, blunt-headed hammer and a chisel with a large cap for striking. Next to them was an irregular-shaped shard of stone with the face and flowing hair of a young woman carved on it. The goddess of the grotto, Chris thought.

"Do you like the coffee?" the don asked, unfazed by Chris's silence. Seemingly unfazed.

"It's very good."

"You have two children?"

"Yes."

"Don DiGiglio's grandchildren."

"Yes."

"Tell me why you are here."

"One of my ship's captains," Chris replied, his voice, and words, measured, "hired a young Ukrainian to make contact with my son. He was to offer him stolen diamonds for sale. The captain said that the offer was from you."

The old Russian nodded, his face unreadable, as still as the water in the middle of the pond.

"If my son bought the diamonds," Chris continued, "the money was meant to be traceable to him, and through him to me, to connect me and my family to something that was going to happen, a connection that would have made life very difficult for me, for my entire family."

"And your son's name?"

"Matthew."

Marchenko smiled; a thousand wrinkles briefly appeared on a face that a moment before had been as smooth as ice and almost as white. "The apostle John lived in Ephesus," he said, the smile gone, his face alabaster again. "In 90 A.D. And Mary, she died here. Who is Matthew, in your family?"

"No one," Chris answered, understanding the question immediately. "We liked the name, my wife and I."

"Don DiGiglio's daughter."

"Yes."

"Your ex-wife."

"Yes."

"America."

"America," Chris said, smiling very faintly, with his eyes only, thinking of his father, Joseph, who should have had the honor of being the namesake of Chris's first son. *No, Don Marchenko, America—the modern world—was not the reason for this slight, but perhaps you know that already.*

"Have you spoken to your captain?" the Russian asked.

"He's been killed."

"By whom?"

"Whoever hired him to hire the Ukrainian."

"And this is where I come in."

"Yes."

"What exactly do you want from me?"

"A man named Marko Dravic has approached me. A Russian businessman. He got my attention by briefly abducting my daughter. I need to know if he is the originator of the diamond ploy. Also, who he works for."

"Who he works for?"

"Yes."

"What did he want of you?"

"He asked me to go to Prague, to help the Czechs stop a terrorist attack. He says the Russians won't be trusted in Prague. He says he is just a businessman who has been asked by his government to approach me."

"What kind of attack?"

"He didn't say."

"The Russians?"

"GRU."

"Will you go?"

"Yes."

The old man got up slowly, rising—unfolding it seemed to Chris—to his full height of no more than five and a half feet. He was rail thin. Taking a thick stick from the ground, he poked it into the pond and swirled it around, creating concentric ripples that went forth and faded as they reached the far bank. These small marching waves glistened as they caught the morning sun.

"I love this place," the don said, turning and facing Chris, holding the mud-coated stick out before him like a baton, lining it up with Chris's face. "I will die here soon. But I have children and grandchildren, and men who have sworn their lives to me."

"I am asking a lot," Chris said, "I realize that."

"How do you know it wasn't me who hired the Ukrainian?" the don said. "That Dravic is not my man."

"You would not have put the grandchildren of Anthony DiGiglio in harm's way."

Marchenko smiled his wrinkled smile again, then looked closely at Chris. "You know, Christoff," he said, "the Turks used to fabricate terrorist attacks by the Greeks as a way of keeping their people stirred up and of course distracted. Now the Israelis are the devils. Sometimes the attacks are real, with evidence left pointing to Tel Aviv. It's what governments do in this part of the world. But only *governments* retaliate against other governments."

Chris remained silent. He got the point. The price for Marchenko's help would be very high.

"Have you tried yourself?" the don asked.

"Yes. But no luck. My people in Moscow have found nothing and time is running out."

"Where does he go?"

"To his office, to church."

"He goes to mass on Sundays?"

"No, he visits at random times."

"Which church?"

"The Cathedral of Christ the Savior in Moscow."

"Does he go alone?"

"We believe so."

"How much time do I have?"

"The attack is supposed to occur on September eleven."

"Thirteen days."

Chris nodded. "Thirteen days."

"Do you know of the Emperor Theodosius?" the don asked.

"No," Chris answered.

"He built a stone wall around Constantinople, fifteen hundred years ago. Some of it now encloses us here." Marchenko gazed at the parts of the wall around them that were not covered by vines, his light, intelligent eyes seeming to look into the past. "They are careless with their treasures, the Turks, now that they are an Islamist state. They disdain anything not Muslim." The don, a wry smile on his face, threw the muddy stick into the pond, then strode to the stone slab. Swiftly and with surprising ease and grace, he lifted the hammer, placed the chisel vertically on the goddess's face and cleaved her in half. "I will do as you ask. Take this," he said, handing half of the shard to Chris, leaving the other half on the slab. "The person with the other half will tell you what I have been able to discover."

"Thank you for seeing me. And for your help," Chris said, rising, "I am in your debt. When this is over, you may call on me at any time."

∧ ∧ ∧ ∧ ∧

Chris was relieved to see Costa Vasiliou watching from the stern rail as the launch approached *Eleftheria* at anchor in Samos's Karlovassi Harbor. He had entered Turkey illegally, and, though Chris had been received politely by Marchenko in his den, the Russian don was nevertheless a lion, old but far from toothless. Chris had not slept well on the overnight cruise from

Skopelos, and now, gripping Costa's large brown hand as he was helped aboard, he was tired.

"Did you make the call, Costa?" he asked, standing next to his captain at the rail, watching the launch being lifted onto the deck.

"Yes."

"Thank you. I will fly to Prague from Skiathos tonight."

"I will make the arrangements. Are you going alone?"

"Matt will come with me. Tess will fly separately. Send two of your men with her, the ones watching her now. Put her in the Europa. They are not to leave her until I say so."

Costa nodded. "How was Turkey?"

Not, *how was the don?* Or, *how did your business go?* How was *Turkey?* This was Costa's one weakness, his hatred of the Turks. Christina hated them even more, if that were possible.

"I am glad to be back on Greek soil."

Costa smiled, his white teeth brilliant against the blue-water tan of his face.

"And Marchenko?" he asked.

"Don Marchenko has made an idol of himself," Chris replied. "It is the great sin of our age."

"No one above God, no *thing* above God."

"Yes."

"Shall I continue to watch Mr. Dravic?"

Neither Costa nor Max French had been able to discover who Marko Dravic was. *Frie Markit* was registered in the Cayman Islands in the name of a Swiss corporation. There was no getting behind those curtains without Mr. White's help, and Chris did not want that help.

"Tell me: when he goes to the Cathedral in Moscow, what does he do?"

"He is met by an old woman, who escorts him through a door behind the altar."

"Where your people cannot follow."

"Yes. It is perhaps a private chapel. Or meeting place."

"Do you have pictures of the people who enter before him?"

"No, we followed him there."

"Are there other entrances?"

"Several."

"Who is the bishop there?"

"Bishop Josef Bukov."

"Check him out."

"I will. Shall I continue following Dravic?"

"No, it is not necessary. Have last night's pictures arrived?"

"They came in while you were ashore."

"Put the prints in my briefcase. I will look at them on the plane."

25.

Skiathos, August 29, 2012, 8:00 p.m.

"Tell me what happened," Chris said.

Matt had been waiting for this question for the past two days, unnerved by how long it took his father to ask it. They were seated on plush leather swivel chairs in the lounge area amidships of a corporate jet, a twin-engine Gulfstream, as it stood on the tarmac at the airport on the island of Skiathos. A cable news program was being broadcast on two high definition televisions mounted on the walls above them; the newsreader, a handsome middle-aged man, looked grim as he spoke of Greece's financial crisis. There will be a delay, the captain had told them when they boarded, perhaps thirty minutes, nothing unusual. The hostess, in a simple black skirt and white blouse, with an onyx pin on it that said, *Hellenic Waste Management,* served them sparkling water and retreated through the door that led to the service area at the rear of the plane. The six passenger seats, also buttery-looking leather, were empty.

"The guy pulled a gun," Matt said, thinking of the days when he was thirteen and thought that Mafia violence was cool. "He had already hit her with a bat. I saw the bruise. He was drunk, or high on something."

"So it was self-defense? Him or you?"

"Yes."

Silence.

"What did he look like?"

"A mess, like he'd been up all night drinking, or drugging, probably both."

"Describe him."

"Six-three, two-thirty, cut, tattooed, long greasy hair."

"How long?"

"Almost to his shoulders."

"Where were the tattoos?"

"His forearms."

"Of what?"

Matt stopped to think. "I can't remember," he said finally.

"What did he say?"

"He asked me who I was. *Who the fuck are you?* he said, when I told him. *I want to see my kids.*"

Chris nodded.

"Don't ask me the color of his eyes, Dad," Matt said, half smiling. "I don't know."

"And the woman? Anna." Chris said. "Where is she now?"

"She's here."

"You brought her here?"

"Yes."

"Where is she?"

"In town, in a hotel."

"How old is she?"

"How old is she?"

"Yes."

"Thirty-two."

"The kids, are they here too?"

"Yes."

Matt watched his father absorb all this, his face unreadable.

"I was crazy about your mother when we first met."

Matt said nothing. What could he say to that?

"Why did you bring her?" Chris asked. "Are you worried about their safety?"

"Yes. I was afraid friends of Nico would want revenge, or come after her looking for the money."

"Max says she's a Czech national. When did she come to the U.S.?"

"When she was eighteen."

"She's fluent in Czech, I take it. Anything else? Czech kids learned Russian in grammar school."

"I don't know."

"What's her story?"

"Her father worked in the underground against the Russians. He was arrested, tortured and killed when Anna was ten. Her mother had died earlier. She came to the U.S. on a work visa when she was eighteen, then married Cavanagh."

"What was the father's name?"

"The full name, I don't know. Cervenka, I assume."

"Have you checked out her story?"

"Dad..."

"I'll do it."

Chris picked his cell phone up from the coffee table between them and dialed a number. "Costa," he said after a moment or two. "Where are you?" Chris listened for the time it took Costa to answer, then said, "Turn around. Matt will meet you in the harbor." Then to Matt: "Take Costa and pick up Anna and the kids. Drop the kids off to Christina, bring Anna here. She'll come with us.

"Why?"

"She speaks Czech, she knows the city. My bet is she speaks Russian too. She'll blend in. I may need someone like that."

"She's a civilian. She's completely innocent."

Chris did not respond to this immediately. His face was set at an angle that prevented Matt from seeing his eyes. *What's he thinking? He never thinks just nothing. It's always something.*

"No one's completely innocent, Matt," Chris said finally, turning to face his son.

"You may be right," Matt said, thinking of Anna, of how she would react to another abrupt move, knowing she would have no choice. Once Uncle Frank DiGiglio's two farmers showed up and took Skip Cavanagh's body away, while she watched, even offering them coffee, she had crossed the line into the parallel world where the Chris Massi's, the Max French's, the Frank DiGiglio's—and now the Matt Massi's—lived and worked, interacting with but never re-joining the world where normal people, civilians, lived their lives, with only sins of the flesh and spirit to haunt them, not murder or worse.

"What about the two wounds?" Chris Massi asked. "Uncle Frank said there were two wounds. Did you have to shoot him twice."

"Yes, I did," Matt replied without hesitation, thinking, *I should have known he'd speak to Frank.* And then a worse thought: *he knows I'm lying.* "I was nervous. I missed low with the first shot."

"How did it feel?" Chris asked.

"I don't know. Inevitable."

26.

Prague, September 1, 2012, 2:00 p.m.

Of the women whose pictures he had fallen in love with, Tess Massi was the first Max French had spent any time with. Or even met for that matter. He had never been formally introduced to the beautiful redhead, Megan Nolan, nor could you call the five minutes he was in her presence before she was killed in an abandoned hunting lodge as having spent time with her. The same went for Jeanne-Claude Robiana, the woman who had slowly killed her husband with rat poison in Paris. A reporter then, he had covered her arrest and attended every minute of her trial, but there was all that distance between them. Now he found himself walking over the Charles Bridge on a beautiful late summer day with Tess Massi, feeling guilty about the photograph of her he kept in his jacket pocket, and shy to the point of *psychosomatic-muteness*, a term used by psychiatrists to describe the shell he went into after watching his step-father kill his mother when he was thirteen.

"Max," Tess said.

"Sorry, yes?"

"Are you with me?"

"Yes, of course."

"You were drifting."

"No, I was assessing our situation."

"What situation?"

"The pedestrians around us, the vendors, the guy on stilts with the striped pants and wig, the boat that just passed under the bridge."

This was not a lie. Situational awareness was for Max a near automatic, near constant function of his brain and his senses. At the same time as he was re-membering the term psychosomatic muteness, he was seeing and hearing the man on the sightseeing boat, in a blue vest and bowtie, microphone in hand, describ-ing the sights of Prague to his passengers. *The Charles Bridge with its historic Gothic Towers was built in the fourteenth and fifteenth centuries. Construction began in 1347 under the auspices of King Charles IV...* he remem-bered hearing.

Tess, absorbing this, remained silent, which was fine with Max, but alas, not only was Tess beautiful, she was also normal in all respects, including her eagerness to talk to the man who would be watching over her un-til she left Prague. *The mysterious Max French*, she had said when they were introduced, *at last*. This did not bode well, and now here he was.

"Is that something I'll learn how to do in Arizona?" she asked.

"Yes."

"My father said you teach there."

"Sometimes."

"I'm sorry I forced you to do this."

"You mean take a walk?"

"Yes."

"You have to get out."

"You could have sent one of the other guys."

"No, I couldn't." If you get hurt or taken, I'm a dead man, so no, it has to be me who takes the two walks a day with you.

"Let's start now," Tess said.

"Start what?"

"My training."

"Tess...can I call you Tess?"

A second of silence. Two seconds. The man on the stilts was a woman. She had breasts. He had given her a wide berth and seen their profile under her bright red shirt. She was behind them now, handing a balloon to a small child.

"Of course," Tess said.

Silence. The bridge was fine.

"Max."

"Yes?"

"Can we start now? I mean it."

"The person on the stilts," Max said. "Was it a man or a woman?"

"I don't know. A man I assume."

"Did you notice the wig?"

"How could I miss it?"

"What color?"

"Purple."

"It was a woman. What would you do if she approached us?" Tess turned to look back at the stilt person, now some twenty yards away.

"I don't know?"

"Move to the side. And if she reached into her pants pocket?"

Silence.

"Go low. Knock her off her stilts. Pull your weapon. Point it at her head from behind."

"Max, are you serious?"

"Yes and no."

"You sound like my father."

I'm forty-five, Max thought, *old enough to be your father. And of course your father...well, I work for him.* As he thought this, Max could not stop himself from thinking about the sound of his name coming from Tess's lips, of how her voice made such a stupid name sound...sound what? *Normal, a nice name for a man to have. Fuck. Stop it, Max.*

"That's a compliment," Max said.

"What, that you sound like my father?"

"Yes."

"Tell me about Arizona. I'm nervous about what to expect. Very nervous."

"Everyone there will be nervous. Even your instructors."

"Why?"

"I'll tell you one overall concept. So that you won't be killed, err on the side of killing."

Silence.

"Do you know how to use a knife?"

"No, of course not."

"Tomorrow, instead of taking a walk I'll teach you the fundamentals." *The proximity will kill me, but I'll do it.*

"Good, thank you."

"No problem."

"Max?"

"Yes?"

"What happened? Why are you so shy?'

Max's throat suddenly became very dry. He stopped walking. With some effort, he worked up some saliva and swallowed. He opened his mouth to talk, but nothing came out.

"Don't answer," Tess said, taking his arm and getting them walking again. "What kind of knife will we start with?"

27.

Prague, September 1, 2012, 6:00 p.m.

"Is this it?" Matt asked.

Anna did not answer. She had her hair pulled back in a ponytail and was wearing no makeup but, standing there in the late-day sunlight, staring at the tiny house and barren front yard, the site of the event that changed her life in ways he could only imagine, she looked more starkly beautiful than ever. Matt had linked pain and wisdom before in his mind, but never pain and beauty. Until today.

"Yes," she said, finally. "This is it."

Matt knew enough to say nothing. *Silence is never inaccurate* was another one of his father's admonitions. *Nor embarrassing or stupid,* he thought.

"What are you thinking?" Anna asked.

"Only of you."

"Why are we here, Teo?"

"In Prague, you mean?"

"Yes."

"I don't know. I'm not sure."

"I do. It is fate that brought me here. I fled Prague as soon as I legally could. I wanted nothing to do with the Czechs, the people who allowed themselves to be enslaved, who allowed my father to be tortured and killed because he was fighting for their freedom. And now I am back. How strange."

"It can't be circumvented, or thwarted," Matt said, "no matter how you try."

"My fate."

"Yours, mine, everyone's, yes."

"What is it? My fate."

Matt shrugged. "My father speaks of inevitability all the time, Anna. He had me memorize *Antigone* when I was fifteen. 'It will reveal itself,' he used to say. Be ready.'"

"Your father wants my help."

"Yes."

"Perhaps your father can help *me*."

"How?"

"I would like to find Mr. Blond Man."

"Anna..."

"I thought I saw him today, getting into a limousine near our hotel."

Silence.

"I'm not crazy. He's here, Matt. I can feel it."

"What would you do if you found him?"

"I would kill him of course, with your help."

"Anna..."

"Many former *Kumunists* have blended back in, have gotten away with their murders and their tortures. They are alive and happy. My father is dead."

"When did you get this idea?"

"On the plane."

"Anna..."

"We have already killed one person who deserved to die, you and I," Anna said. "And who deserves more to die than Mr. Blond Man? It is what your grandfather did, is it not? Joseph Massi, Sr?"

"How do you know about him?"

"It doesn't matter, Teo. What matters is that his blood is in your veins, and my father's blood is in mine."

28.

Prague, September 1, 2012, 7:05 p.m.

Mr. Massi,

I will be in the lobby this evening at 7:00 p.m., sitting near the fountain. I will be wearing a yellow flowered print dress. I have the other half of an icon that you will recognize.

Valentina Petrov

This note was in an inside pocket of Chris Massi's linen sport jacket as he sat across from Valentina Petrov in a plush chair in the sunken living room of his penthouse suite at Prague's Europa Hotel. The wall nearest to them was floor-to-ceiling glass, the view twenty stories below to Wenceslas Square and the Charles Bridge in the distance postcard perfect. As the sun set, lights were twinkling on in a city that in Chris's view matched Paris in its beauty and overmatched it, by far, in its heart.

"You are a cautious man," Ms. Petrov said.

"I try to be," Chris replied, acknowledging that the woman sitting across from him was referring to the fact that he had not met her in the lobby, but had sent two of the hotel's security men to escort her to his apartment.

"What if I had refused?" she asked.

"They were told not to take no for an answer."

"Someone may have noticed."

"I own this hotel," Chris replied. "People here see what I want them to see, no more."

This statement produced a slight upward tilt of Valentina Petrov's chin, a movement that enhanced the Russian woman's great, dark beauty, softly modeled at that moment by the flickering light from a group of candles on the glass coffee table between them. Next to them were the two pieces of Don Marchenko's stone goddess, and next to them two fluted glasses and a bottle of Cristal Champagne on ice in a silver bucket.

"Shall we drink?" Chris said, lifting the champagne and filling the glasses. "I appreciate your help in this matter." He lifted his glass and watched as Ms. Petrov placed a napkin on the stem of hers and lifted it. "Thank you," he said.

"You are welcome."

They drank.

"Don Marchenko is lucky to have such a beautiful employee," said Chris, setting his glass down.

"I am not an employee," Valentina Petrov replied. "But I admit, he has been good to my family and I am happy to carry a message for him from time to time if he asks."

"He is a great man," Chris said. "What has he done for you and your family?"

"He and my grandfather were boyhood friends in Odessa. When my grandfather died young, Don Marchenko helped support the family. He sent my father to America to college and medical school."

"As I say, a great man."

"You remind me of him," Miss Petrov said. "Very much."

"Thank you. That is a great compliment."

"Do you want to hear his message?"

"Not yet," Chris answered. "Do you know your Russian history?"

"Russian history?"

"Yes, this champagne, for example, was first produced by Louis Roderer for Czar Nicholas. Later, Alexander II insisted it come in clear bottles with flat bottoms."

"Why?"

"He was afraid someone would smuggle a bomb in it."

"Better to be a poor nobody," Valentina said, "than a czar worried about assassination all the time."

"Not in 19th century Russia."

"He *was* assassinated though, was he not?" Valentina asked.

"Yes," Chris replied. "In 1881, despite all his precautions. Do you know why?"

"No, I'm afraid not. The czars are still not much in favor in Mother Russia."

"Your present prime minister is pretty much a czar, is he not?"

"We have many freedoms."

"Have I insulted you?"

"No, I am not naïve, but communism was much worse."

"How did you learn to speak such perfect English?"

"My father hired private tutors for my brother and me. He was two, I was three."

"Shall we speak more English at dinner tomorrow?" said Chris. "Say ten o'clock at the restaurant here?"

"I would enjoy that. Shall I wait till then to give you Don Marchenko's message?"

"No, tell me now. What does he say?"

"That Mr. Dravic is not connected to the diamonds. That the Kremlin's concerns about something happening in Prague are legitimate. That the deadline remains September eleven."

"Thank you, Valentina," Chris said. "May I call you Valentina?"

"Of course."

"When will you see Don Marchenko again?" he asked.

"It is rare that I see him."

"Do you know what the *something* is that might be happening in Prague?"

"Of course not."

"Did you come to Prague just to see me?"

"My brother is here to tape a television show. I help him organize his life."

"What kind of television show?"

"He is a priest who is much in demand for his political views."

"Which are?"

"Conservative. Anti-communist."

"He must be good looking and well-spoken, like his sister."

Valentina did not reply.

"Charismatic, perhaps," Chris said.

"Yes," the Russian woman said. "He is that."

"Please ask him to join us tomorrow night. He sounds very interesting."

"I will."

Chris rose and watched as Valentina placed her glass, with the napkin still wrapped around its stem, on the coffee table, and got to her feet as well.

"Alexander II was killed by a bomb in St. Petersburg," Chris said. "Thrown by a fanatic from The Peoples Will."

"The Peoples Will?"

"Terrorists fomenting a peasants revolution, which Lenin and the Bolsheviks accomplished in 1917."

"You *do* know Russian history."

"It's a hobby."

"A hobby. And what is it that you do?"

"It will bore you, I promise," Chris replied, "but I will tell you tomorrow night."

∧ ∧ ∧ ∧ ∧

When she was gone, Chris lifted the napkin from Valentina Petrov's champagne glass, then raised the glass to a nearby lamp to inspect it. As he was putting it down, his cell phone rang. Costa, he said to himself, when he retrieved the phone from his jacket's inside pocket and saw the ID number on the screen. He touched the answer bar.

"Yes," he said.

"Anadochos."

"Costa."

"Josef Bukov was at Octha in 1979. He washed out. He is the bishop."

"Who else was there that year, and the years before and after?"

"I will find out."

"Thank you. One more thing."

"Of course."

"Valentina Petrov, age: mid-thirties, born Odessa. She has a brother who is a priest and is on television."

"Where is she now?"

"Here in Prague."

"I will do my best."

"Thank you."

29.

Prague, September 3, 2012, 1:00 a.m.

Chris asked no questions at dinner. Inquisition, no matter with what finesse it was done, would be a red flag to a professional, which Chris assumed Valentina Petrov was. Her brother he was not so sure of. Perhaps he was a crusading priest and perhaps not. Conversation was light and breezy, but nevertheless revealing. Father Nicholei was officially assigned to Christ The Savior, Russia's great national cathedral, though his primary work was to disseminate the church's traditional values. This he managed to do with great success with the help of Valentina, who had worked for years as a newscaster on Russian television. They loved him in Central Europe's capitals, where communism was hated and the church was still regarded with reverence and respect.

When Valentina, in a simple black evening dress with diamonds at her throat and ears, went off to powder her nose before the coffee arrived, Chris decided he could be a little less cautious. "She is beautiful," he said, as they watched her wind her way through the quiet and beautifully appointed restaurant to the ladies room behind the bar area.

"She is," the handsome young priest replied.

"And a great help to you."

"Yes, devoted."

"You have no pastoral duties?"

"No."

"You speak to a much wider audience."

"Yes, you could say that."

"Do you live on the cathedral grounds?"

"Yes, in the residence on Lenivka Street."

"I would like to see it one day."

"I will give you a tour."

"I would like that. I've read that the original cathedral, the one that Stalin tore down, had twenty tons of gold in the dome."

"Alas, Stalin built several dachas with it."

"And that it had underground passages leading to the Kremlin and the czars's residences."

"Yes, many are still there, though I doubt they are used much, if at all."

"I saw you on television tonight, Father."

"You did? Do you speak Czech, Mr. Massi?" the young priest asked, his dark eyebrows raised.

"No, it was in English. I have Dual Sound software on my computer."

"Amazing. How did I do?"

"You were quite critical of Mr. Putin."

"Ah yes, the Pussy Riot Girls, protesting at the cathedral. Are you surprised?"

"They want Putin thrown out of office."

"They are free, in my opinion, to say so."

"Do you say the same things in Moscow?"

"Yes, of course."

"I assumed you would stick to safe subjects, like abortion and homosexuality."

"You were wrong in this instance."

"Shall I be frank?"

"Please."

"I did not think people were allowed to disagree with Putin, especially on television, especially a priest."

"A priest? Why?"

"The church supported Putin in both of his elections. It has harshly condemned the three young girls. Does your bishop support you?"

"My bishop?"

"Yes, Father Bukov."

"You seem to know a lot about us, Mr. Massi."

"I am an amateur historian. But I will expose my ignorance if I continue. I will change the subject. Does your father still practice medicine?"

Father Nicholas was silent as he pondered this abrupt turn in the conversation. He glanced at Chris for a second, the first time, Chris noted, thus far in the evening that he had looked with care in his direction. *Yes Father, do not trust me.*

"Yes," the priest replied finally, "he is a surgeon in Odessa."

Chris nodded. "At which hospital?"

"The Medeyev Clinic. Do you know Odessa?"

"It is a great port city," Chris answered. "I own ships that stop there frequently."

"Do you own a hotel there as well?"

"No, this and the Intercontinental in Budapest are my only hotels." Then, looking over the priest's shoulder and nodding, Chris said, "Here is your beautiful and devoted sister."

They rose as Valentina arrived, her diamonds glittering even in the room's subdued lighting. They sat again after, with Chris's courtly assistance, she had retaken her seat.

∧ ∧ ∧ ∧ ∧

"I have surprised myself," Valentina Petrov said.

"What do you mean?" Chris Massi asked. "By being here with me?"

"Yes. We've just met, and here I am in your beautiful penthouse with the lights low and candles burning."

They were seated in the same chairs in Chris's suite as the evening before. The same candles were burning in an otherwise nearly dark room. A bottle of very good Cognac and two half-full snifters sat near the candles.

"Fire, water," Chris said, "I like them around me. In Skopelos I have a fountain in the center atrium that is often the only music we need."

"Elemental."

"Yes, like you."

"Like me?"

"I meet many women, Valentina. Most are ungrounded, afraid."

"Who is *we*?"

"In Skopelos?"

"Yes."

"My staff and me. My children when they visit." Chris paused, then continued, "you need not stay long."

"I am here," Valentina said. "I have crossed the Rubicon, as they say. If I stay ten minutes or ten hours, it doesn't matter."

"So you're here to conquer me, as Caesar did Gaul?"

"You are not conquerable, Don Massi, and that is most attractive, most *elementally* attractive, to a woman."

"You are not relaxed, though. I can tell."

"Did you mean it when you said people here see only what you want them to see?"

"My private elevator is guarded around the clock," Chris answered. "The men who escorted you up here are professionals."

"Yes, but when I leave...?"

"How did you exit last night?"

"I was blindfolded, but I suppose you know that."

"Yes, a necessary precaution."

"They took me out by way of an office building on the block behind."

"You can relax. I bought this hotel with that kind of ingress and egress in mind. The office building is not the only one. Are you concerned about appearances? Your brother? Is that it?"

"I never...I don't do this as a rule, and I never do this when I travel with him."

"He can't be tainted you mean."

"Yes. Correct."

"But you are here."

"You noticed."

"Why?"

"You must know how attractive you are. I am not a *girl* that you feel you must be...*careful* with. Do you find *me* attractive?"

Chris did not answer immediately. He allowed himself to look carefully, for the first time, at Valentina Petrov. What he saw—the wide-apart dark eyes lit with desire, the creamy skin, the sensuous mouth, the hardness at the core of her—brought to mind the complicated nature of his sexual life, of its occasional ravenous affairs separated by long intervals of austerity and self-denial. This was as distinct from his love life, which had included only two women, his ex-wife and an ex-girlfriend who had saved his life, both icons locked in a room he could never re-enter. He could feel himself getting aroused. *Thank God*, he thought, *it's been too long.*

He rose then, and went to sit on the wide cushioned arm of Valentina's chair. She turned to face him, but he put his hands on her bare shoulders and turned her away from him. On the back of her right shoulder was a small amoeba-shaped patch of lighter-colored flesh, where perhaps a tattoo had been surgically erased or a vaccination had left its mark. He bent and kissed this patch and then, lifting her long hair, brushed his lips against the back of her neck, lingering for a second, breathing in her faint but sweet and heady perfume. Then he sat up and slowly unzipped the back of her dress, revealing a black strapless bra, which he unhooked. Reaching around he pulled the top of her dress and her bra down to her waist at the same time, then turned her firmly back to him. Hovering a foot or so above her, her head tilted up to face him, he looked down into her eyes and reached for her heavy breasts and caressed and kneaded them. As he did this he kept his eyes locked on hers and felt himself get very hard when he saw the half dazed, half pleading look in them. Taking her hand he led her into the bedroom where he pulled open the wall-to-ceiling drapes so that the lights of Prague, like eyes in the night, could watch them making love, and the full moon hanging over the Charles Bridge could bathe them with its silvery, elemental light.

30.

Prague, September 3, 2012, 7:00 a.m.

"Are we clean, Mr. Kovarik?"

"Yes. Now tell me, why am I here?"

"Here," Chris said, handing Stefan Kovarik an eight-by-ten color photograph of a pale man, in his fifties, in a stylish suit, sitting in the lounge of a bar or restaurant, a drink in front of him, dim light, possibly from a streetlight, filtering through large draped windows at his back.

"Who is this?" the Czech asked.

"His name is Marko Dravic. He is a Russian businessman. Or so he claims. He approached me last week to tell me that the Kremlin has intelligence regarding an attack in Prague, in Wenceslas Square, on September eleven. He asked me to let SIS know. The Russians want to help, he claimed, but they believe that your government would not take them seriously if they approached you directly."

"Utter nonsense."

"I agree. Still, have you heard anything?"

"We hear things all the time."

"I'm sure you do, but as to next Tuesday, the eleventh?"

"Max said something about the Chechans."

Chris raised his eyebrows, elongating as he did the lightning bolt between his eyes. When he did this he could feel the scar tissue stretching, a silent reminder of his encounter with the Russian he had come to call the Wolf. The scar didn't bother him, but the memory of the saliva on his face did. "You didn't answer my question," he said, his voice neutral, but not quite friendly.

"Who are you, Mr. Massi?" Kovarik asked. "We have you categorized as an immensely wealthy, highly sophisticated Mafia boss."

"And Max?" Chris asked. "How have you categorized him?"

"I am here because of him."

"We're old friends," Chris said.

"I understand, but..."

"Let me make myself as clear as I can," Chris said, as Kovarik's voice trailed off. "Max works for me. If I told him to kill you and your assistant right now, he would do it without the slightest hesitation. Do you understand?"

Chris kept his eyes on Kovarik while the Czech agent thought this over, and Max, who had not said a word after introducing Kovarik and his associate, cleared his throat.

"Whoever you are, your cover is very good," Kovarik said.

"Not good enough," Chris said. "Dravic didn't pick me out of the phonebook." Throughout this exchange, Chris's tone of voice had remained not friendly but not hostile, his face, except for his eyes, expressionless. It was the look in these dark, almost black eyes, that he knew had stopped Kovarik in mid-sentence.

"No," the Czech said.

"You kicked the Russians out," Chris continued, "but don't underestimate them. They're very good at this. Something very nasty is about to happen. I can feel it in my bones. My Sicilian bones."

Kovarik nodded. His assistant, a young technician, had pushed himself as far back in his chair as he could. He had seen the look in Chris's eyes as well, and did not want this Max French person to end his life before it had really begun.

"So," Chris said. "We will divert for a second. Dravic *did* mention Caucasus Emirates, as Max *did* in fact tell you. Are they on your radar?"

"No."

"Nothing?"

"We have been watching two Russian couples who are here on work visas."

"Why?"

"We don't think they are Russian."

"Why?"

"We profile, and we have a facial scanner at the airport that tells us generally where people have their roots. Their blood roots."

"Did they come up as Chechan?"

"Yes."

"Why are they here?"

"They are members of Russia's delegation to the UN's Human Rights Council. The fall council session is underway here."

"What have they been doing?"

"Nothing. Working, having dinner out."

"Visitors?"

"They live in a high-rise, so no. We have a few pictures of them out with friends. I'll send them to you."

"What about the street entrance, the lobby, the elevators?"

"Nothing. We have lots of pictures, which we've run through our computers as well as Europol's, but no matches, no one on our radar or even close."

"I'd like the whole file."

"Of course." Kovarik nodded to his assistant, who nodded back.

Chris had risen early to swim in the penthouse's pool, first calling Max to arrange this meeting with Stefan Kovarik, who was ostensibly the owner of an English language school in the office building behind the Europa, but in reality worked for SIS, the Czech equivalent of the CIA. His associate, a teacher at the school, had just swept the penthouse for bugs. Chris was dressed casually, in tan slacks and a lightweight navy blue sweater over a snow-white collared shirt. His black hair was still wet from his swim and shower, a morning ritual, an ablution of sorts that he tried to perform wherever he was in the world.

They were sitting, Chris and Max facing Kovarik and his assistant, in a quiet room off of Chris's study that had a view straight down the café- and hotel-lined Vaclavske Namesti to the Wenceslas Monument and the National Museum. The famous square and the broad avenue were nearly empty. A lone street cleaner and a couple of waiters setting outdoor tables for early coffee drinkers and tourists were going about their business, their deliberate movements accentuating rather than marring the stillness. In the pink early morning air, there hovered the spirits—their presence felt by all Czechs as a chill down the spine—of the crowds of people that had animated, and immortalized, the square with cries of freedom in November, 1989.

"Is anything happening in the square on the eleventh?" Chris asked.

"The national museum has been closed," Kovarik replied, "undergoing an extensive renovation. The ribbon-cutting for the reopening is that day and there is an American exhibition that will debut."

"What time?"

"One p.m."

"Who will cut the ribbon?"

"President Klaus. I believe Mrs. Clinton will be present."

All were silent as this sunk in.

"What exactly is the intelligence that the Russians have?" Kovarik asked.

"I don't know," Chris replied. "I was told that when I arrived in Prague I was to call a certain number to arrange a meeting."

"Have you?"

"Yes."

"And?"

"I have been invited to a reception for the new Iranian ambassador at the Russian Embassy on Friday night. I assume someone will approach me."

"The Jiri Popper House," Kovarik said. "His daughter is suing to get it back."

"I wish her luck," Chris said. He knew the history of Jiri Popper, the wealthy Jewish businessman, whose elegant mansion in the leafy Bubenic section of Prague had been confiscated by the Germans in the war and the Russians afterward. He had met Popper's daughter, Lisbeth, at a reception in New York in 2009 and later donated to her legal fund.

"Tell me, Mr. Massi," Kovarik went on, "on what basis would you be invited to this reception?"

"I deliver crude oil all over the Mediterranean. I have Russian clients."

Kovarik, with short sandy hair, young for a man in such a position, no more than thirty-five, turned to his left to look down at Wenceslas Square. Turning back, he pulled a pack of cigarettes and a gold lighter from a front pocket of his sport jacket. "May I?"

"Yes, be my guest," Chris answered.

The Czech intelligence agent tapped a cigarette from the pack, a Murad, with thin blue stripes above the filter, lit it, inhaled, and blew out the chalky gray smoke. "I do not understand," he said, "why the Kremlin feels the need for you to be involved."

"I don't either," Chris said, "but I plan on finding out."

"Shall I contact them?"

"No, I suggest we wait."

"Have you dealt with the Russians on this level?" Kovarik asked.

"No."

"Do they have a reason to want to harm you?"

"Not that I know of."

Neither of these answers was true, but Chris did not want Kovarik to know more about him than was absolutely necessary. He knew more than enough already.

"I take it you've done this kind of thing before, Mr. Massi."

"I have."

"I can't help you inside the Russian embassy."

"Max will be with me."

"Does it occur to you that *you* are the target? Or that you are being set up for something?"

"Yes."

"But you have no idea why."

"Correct."

"Of course I don't believe you."

"I understand. It is your job to distrust people."

"And to protect my country. If you live through your evening at the Popper House..."

"Yes?"

"You must report directly to me. I am now responsible for this operation."

"Of course."

"You will have no choice in the matter. I say this with respect."

"I understand. Will you do me a favor?"

"If I can."

"Keep an eye on Dravic. Tell me where he's staying."

Kovarik thought this over, then nodded, and said, "Yes, of course."

"Thank you," Chris said. "Please keep Max informed."

The Czech intelligence agent nodded again, then said, "In the meantime I am going to pick up our Chechan love birds. Time is too short for anything else."

Chris would have strung out—and intensified—the surveillance, but time *was* very short. In four days, the American Secretary of State and the Czech president could be killed, on sacred ground no less, with perhaps hundreds of collateral losses, a dagger plunged into the heart of Prague, of the Czech people. If the Chechan couples were professionals, it could take several days— possibly longer, possibly never—to get any useful information out of them. "Show them Dravic's picture," Chris said.

"I will, and I will run it through our system. Have you?"

"Yes. Nothing."

"Until now."

"Yes," Chris said, "until now."

∧ ∧ ∧ ∧ ∧

"I don't see anything," Max French said.

"I don't either," Chris Massi replied. Chris had bid Max stay behind after Kovarik and his assistant left. They were still in the same chairs, but leaning over the coffee table in front of them, staring at another eight-by-ten photograph of Marko Dravic in the lounge of the National Hotel in Moscow. On the right side of this picture was a slightly blurry woman in a black, strapless cocktail dress turning a corner. Just half of her appeared, the rear right. Her black hair was worn up, revealing a diamond earring on her right ear and the back of a glittering diamond necklace at her throat. Max had a magnifying glass in his hand, which he now put down. "That doesn't mean it's not there," he said. "But not to worry, the Company could tell us in a few seconds."

"I don't want them involved."

"Why? If she's GRU or SVR, they'll have a file on her, or they'll open one."

"Talk to Matt. Ask him to get his friend Diego Lopez to do it."

"Chris..."

"They'll ruin her."

"You have other ideas."

"I do."

"Like what?"

"That will be up to her."

Max nodded.

"Offer to help with the Chechans's interrogation," Chris said.

"Don't insist?"

"No. I've insulted Kovarik enough. They're good at it anyway, better than us maybe."

"Anything else?"

"Send Kovarik's surveillance file to Costa. There may be a match. He has the Moscow pictures and the boat pictures."

"Do you want a copy?"

"Yes, and you look at it carefully, too."

"You put a GPS tag on Dravic's yacht?"

"Yes, it's tagged. Costa's people will watch him on shore."

"Someday you'll have to tell me about Costa. There's nothing he can't do or get done."

Chris smiled, remembering the night in Athens seven years ago, Costa lying in a gutter, two men in leather jackets standing over him, pistols pointed at his head. "I will," Chris said, "when you need to know. Just like you'll tell me about yourself, the real Max French, when I need to know."

Now Max smiled, thinking of his secrets, including the pictures in his wallet. "I've been out with Tess," he said, pausing just a beat before continuing, "walking around Prague. She's restless, and nervous about Arizona."

"What would you do if it were your daughter?" Chris asked.

"I'd have killed Dravic."

Chris did not respond.

"But I assume," said Max.

"Assume what?"

"That you're waiting."

"Yes, I'm waiting. I'd like to find out who he works for first, who started all this, who had *me* in mind, and why. Then I'll take care Mr. Dravic, or you will for me."

31.

Prague, September 3, 2012, 8:00 a.m.

"Do you know what quantum entanglement encryption is, Matt?" Max French asked.

"No."

"It's an encryption system based on quantum mechanics."

"Quantum mechanics?"

"Do you know what that is?"

"It's a mathematical description of the dual particle-like and wave-like behavior and interactions of energy and matter."

"Christ, you *do* know."

"It's the end of the line for physics, Max. After quantum mechanics there's God, and scientists don't want to go there. They'd go insane."

"Your father said you were smart."

"Did he?"

"He said you were smart and dumb at the same time, like he was at your age."

"I guess that's a compliment."

"It is, believe me. Here, go to this website." Max handed Matt a small piece of notepaper with a web address and a password written on it. "Put in the password. Download the software. Then send your friend Diego the image. There's a phone app there too. Download it."

"How does it work?"

"If there's an auditor, he gets some kind of believable spam, like a recipe for bread or a picture of a Maserati."

"Is there a footprint? I mean Diego..."

"No, no cyber trail. It's completely locked down. It's all we use, email and cell phone, totally secure."

"If there's an auditor, can you track *him*?"

"No but we're working on it."

"Okay. Where's the image?"

"Here." Max handed Matt a CD.

"And where exactly is this birthmark?"

"Her right shoulder."

"OK."

"Time is short, Matt."

Matt nodded and watched Max let himself out of the hotel room. Then he slipped the CD into his laptop and opened the photograph. As he was looking at it, Anna, naked, with a towel on her head, came out of the bathroom and peered over his shoulder.

"You can't see her face," she said.

"No."

"Who is the man?"

"His name is Marko Dravic. He's the one who kidnapped Tess. But it's the woman that's important."

^ ^ ^ ^ ^

Anna woke up with a start that night. She didn't know why. Had she been dreaming?

She and Matt and Tess were staying in a suite on the same floor as Chris Massi's penthouse at the Europa. It had the same view as the penthouse. She went to the window and pulled the curtains open and looked down at Prague. Yes, she *had* been dreaming—the same recurring dream of her father standing in the snow, ax in hand, looking up at her as she stood at her bedroom window. The same rush of fear that always woke her up. But tonight Mr. Blond Man appeared for the first time ever, his face clear and bright and hard as stone in the winter morning sunlight, her first dream ever of him.

She gazed at the lights of Prague. She had been right. He *was* down there someplace, someplace close. She returned to the bedroom and sat on the edge of the bed.

"Matt," she said, shaking him, knowing now why Joseph Massi, Sr. had chosen Wall Storage to hide his two million dollars, why she had married Skip Cavanagh, why she had shot him, why she had returned to Prague. Matt turned toward her and looked at her.

"What?" he said. "Are you okay?"

"Yes," she replied. "I'm okay."

"What is it?"

"I have to speak to your father."

32.

Prague, September 4, 2012, 6:00 a.m.

The eight men who entered the lobby of the Vinice Residence Towers on Ruska Street looked and acted like commercial air conditioning servicemen. BUDOVICE HVAC was emblazoned in flowing script above the pocket of their navy blue work shirts, and they arrived in bright white vans with the same markings on all sides. As a precaution, earlier that morning, one of them made his way to the roof of the twenty-five story building and disabled the three commercial air handlers that pumped cold or hot air into the tower's two hundred apartments.

The doorman had been told to come in late, the lobby was empty and the ride on the elevator was uneventful. On the way up they pulled their Glock 22s from their tool bags and screwed on silencers. On the twentieth floor, four went to apartment 210 and four to

214. Both doors blew up from within when they shot at the locks, killing four of the servicemen, two at each door. A few minutes passed while the survivors called for help and removed the bodies of their colleagues. When they entered the apartments, they found a man and a woman dead in each one. Small leather pouches worn on the necks of each gave off a bitter almond smell and autopsies done later confirmed death from cyanide poisoning.

33.

Prague, September 4, 2012, 5:00 p.m.

"I talked to Kovarik," Max said. "He thinks they kept the doors rigged whenever they were home."

"That's a lot of trouble."

"They'd rather be dead than tortured."

"Any matches anywhere?" Chris asked.

"One print on one finger matched with an Iranian who had been at Gitmo and released. The other three Kovarik is pretty sure were Caucasus Emirate people."

"Any intel?" Chris said. "There must have been computers, cell phones."

"The cell phones and emails they had been surveilling all along," Max replied. "They're opening up the devices now. They don't expect to find much."

"What's Kovarik's take?"

"He thinks the operation will be aborted."

"Do you agree?"

"Yes," Max answered. "Kovarik has let it out that there was a survivor. The thinking is, if they tried to use a new team, the operation could still be traced to its source through him. They can't take that risk, the puppeteers."

"That makes sense, if this was routine insanity."

"You don't think it is?"

"No. Getting *me* involved makes it different."

"Let's hope you're wrong," Max said. "Kovarik has no other leads."

"I assume the security at the ribbon cutting will be at a very high level."

"Are you kidding?" Max replied. "Crazy high. I mean, *Hillary Clinton*?"

"There's no one else in the city that they know of?"

"No. No leads."

"That doesn't mean they're not out there."

"They're gone by now."

Chris and Max were in the penthouse's living room, sipping coffee. Sunlight was beginning to stream in through the wall-to-ceiling windows behind them, Prague to awaken to another day. On the glass table, next to the silver coffee service, lay an eight-by-ten color photograph of a woman's shoulder. Max picked it up. "What about *her*?" he said.

"I'm seeing her later. We're having dinner."

"Where?"

"Here."

"Double agents are a tricky business, Chris. But you know that."

"I do, but I can't pass up the opportunity. And her mission will be very narrowly defined."

"What?"

"To find one man for me who I believe is embedded somewhere in the Kremlin."

34.

Prague, September 4, 2012, 10:00 p.m.

"Nicolei was disappointed he was not invited. He finds you fascinating."

"I needed to speak to you alone, but he actually can help us."

"Help us?"

Chris handed Valentina Petrov two photographs, the first a close-in image of an amoeba-shaped birthmark on a woman's right shoulder, a portion of a diamond necklace appearing at her neck; the second a full view of the lounge of the National Hotel's bar with Marko Dravic sitting in the center and a partial rear view, slightly blurry, of a woman in a strapless black cocktail dress on the far right. He watched as the beautiful Russian spy took them in. They were sitting in his penthouse, drinking a special vintage Cristal Champagne that he had ordered for the occasion. "Let's toast," he said, lifting his glass, when she looked up at him.

"To what."

"To our joining forces."

"Chris..."

"Yes?"

Valentina shrugged her lovely shoulders.

"I've had the photograph enhanced," Chris said.

"I'm afraid I can be of little help." Another shrug.

Submission, Chris thought. "Was there a drop that night at the National?" he asked.

"Yes."

"What was it?"

"I don't know. A piece of paper I was told I would find in the lobby by the house phone. I didn't read it."

"Do you know Dravic?"

"No."

"Marchenko?"

"No."

"Who gave you the icon?"

"It was in a drop here in Prague, with instructions."

"Which you burned."

"Yes."

Chris sipped his champagne, relieved that he did not have to kill Valentina Petrov.

"You have saved your life," he said, "and your brother's."

"He is not part of this."

"I believe you but he can help."

"How?"

"I would like access to the underground passages between the Kremlin and Christ The Savior."

"Access?"

"Yes."

"Your people?"

"Yes."

Chris noticed the slightest change in Valentina's composed face, a deadening of the eyes that lasted a fraction of a second, the time it took for her to lower and lift her lush lashes. She knew that such access meant only one thing.

"You will live, your brother will live," Chris said. "And perhaps you will both be able to get away. The GRU is nowhere near as good as the KGB was in tracking down traitors, and you will have my help."

Silence.

"Shall we toast?"

Valentina Petrov raised her glass, nodded to Chris, and sipped. Chris did the same.

"Who is it?" she asked.

"Whoever gave you your ultimate orders."

"Do you want the name of my contact?"

"Of course not. He's a drone that would only lead to other drones. He may even be dead."

"How did you get these pictures?"

"I have people there," Chris said. "The same people who will kill you and your brother if you betray me."

"One last question."

"Go ahead."

"Have you ever been in love?"

"Twice. To my ex-wife and to a heroin addict."

"What happened to her, the heroin addict?"

"She's dead."

"Did she betray you?"

"No, she overdosed."

35.

Moscow, September 6, 2012, 8:00 p.m.

"I assume we are aborting," said Marko Dravic.

"You are correct."

"And the meeting as well."

"No, that must go forward. And I want the photograph."

Dravic paused. This was insane.

"Our friends will certainly balk."

"They are not our friends. They are the enemies of our enemy. There is a difference."

And who, then, are our actual friends? Dravic thought, then, out loud, "What shall I tell them?"

"That Fallen Heroes is off but that I want the meeting to take place. Tell them again, no meeting, no oil products, no UN cover."

"They may still refuse. They are exposing one of their masterminds."

"I will keep my word. They will both be starved to death."

"Or start World War Three. The Japanese started World War II because of an oil embargo."

"If they do, we will not be on their side. You can tell them that."

"And Massi, shall I tell him that the operation is off?"

"You can tell him, but he will have surmised it from the botched raid on Ruska Street."

"What if he won't meet with us?"

"We will think of something else. But he will. He smells a rat, he is curious."

"What about the fifth man?"

"I will take care of him."

"I must ask, who is Chris Massi? Why are you doing this?"

"Do you know why Don Marchenko is in our pocket?"

"No."

"Do you think he cut us in on all those credit card millions out of the goodness of his heart?"

"No."

"I did him a favor once in America. I killed his only rival. Massi happened to be there at the time, probably trying to get a piece of our skimming machine business in the U.S. I thought he was dead too, that I had gotten lucky and killed two birds. But I was wrong. He saw my face. He is the only person in the world, besides you, who can identify me."

"You went alone?"

"No, one of our American agents joined me, but he's dead now, of course."

"Does that mean I'm next?"

"We have been friends for forty years. I am Uncle V to your two beautiful children. I cannot imagine you would betray me."

"That will not happen," said Dravic, the message loud and clear that if it did, his children would die. And the Wolf had no children, no friends, no lovers, no one that could be killed in return.

36.

Prague, September 7, 2012, 8:00 p.m.

"Heydrich lived here during the war," Chris said. He and Max French and Anna Cavanagh, his Operations Chief and Administrative Assistant, respectively, were seated on plush easy chairs in a quiet room at the rear of the Jiri Popper House.

"Heydrich?"

"The head of Reich security," Chris said. "Hitler called him the man with the iron heart."

Two of the men seated across from Chris looked at him with blank faces. The third, Marko Dravic, frowned, but then smiled. "Mr. Massi is an amateur historian," he said. "World War Two seems to be his area of special interest."

"We are trying to win a war ourselves," said the man sitting on Dravic's right on a richly patterned damask-covered couch. He had been introduced as Abdo Halevi, an assistant to Syria's oil minister.

"This was probably Heydrich's study," Chris said. "He probably came up with the final solution here. To the *Jewish Question*, as the Nazis liked to put it. The mass murder by gas was his idea."

Now Dravic stopped smiling as silence filled the room. After a beat or two, Max French, seemingly unaware that anything untoward had been said or done, rose from his seat next to Chris and went to a rolling bar near an oversized marble fireplace. "Anyone?" he said when he got there, turning to the men seated across from each other in the center of the large room. No one answered. Chris had a glass of water on a lamp table next to his comfortable, heavily cushioned chair. His reply was to pick it up and sip from it. Anna, gorgeous in a black cocktail dress buttoned low at one side, slung over the opposite shoulder, simply shook her head no. As she did, wisps of her long yellow hair fell over her bare shoulder. *Like strands of liquid gold*, Max thought. *Christ.*

While Max was pouring himself a drink, he kept an eye on the group, noticing that Halevi was saying something in Russian, *sotto voce,* to Dravic, who was smiling warmly to his Syrian friend. *This is just a lighthearted exchange.* Of course, Marko. Seated again, he held out his glass of clear liquid, just water, to each of the men sitting across from him, nodding amiably to each. The amethyst stone on his University of Washington class ring caught the light from the crystal chandelier glittering above them as he did this. Then he drank and placed his glass on the same table as Chris's water.

"Where were we?" Max said.

"We were simply introducing Mr. Halevi and Mr. Behzadi to their new business partner," Dravic said. "Before we got sidetracked."

"And what will your role be?" Chris asked Behzadi, who had been introduced as the security liaison between the Oil Ministry and Syrian Military Intelligence. He had clasped both of his hands around Chris's right hand when they shook hands earlier.

"My people will be present," Behzadi answered, "to ensure that only oil products are off-loaded from your tankers."

"Will my ships be searched?"

"Without doubt."

"Then I'm afraid we can't do business."

Behzadi, more Persian-looking than Syrian, smiled, or grimaced in a way that passed for a smile. "Good, we are done," he said.

Chris got to his feet and Max and Anna followed suit. Everyone was stony-faced as Dravic led them out of the room and then returned, shutting the room's large oak door softly behind him.

∧ ∧ ∧ ∧ ∧

Back in the reception hall, with its thick carpets and glittering chandeliers, Chris turned to Anna and said, "Was that him?"

"Yes," she answered. "That was him."

"What did he say to Halevi?"

"You have been insulted. I apologize, but this will not be forgotten."

"I have spoken to a friend in Czech intelligence," Chris said, nodding. "He tells me that a man matching Dravic's description, a Russian, worked in Prague for the Adamec Interior Ministry from 1985 to 1989. He was probably KGB. His name was Marko Dravnova."

"What did he do?"

"He hunted down members of the resistance."

"And then tortured and killed them."

"Yes. Many good people, men and women."

Anna's face brightened. "He is here," she said. "They can arrest him."

"No, I need Dravic to be free."

"Free? Why? He is a murderer."

"If he is killed, or disappears, it will raise an alarm that I don't want raised."

Silence. Max had slipped away. They were alone.

"Anna," Chris said, taking her gently by the arm and leading her to a small arched alcove where they were in shadow but could see the long rectangular room in all its splendor.

"Yes?" Anna replied.

"Matt has told me what you've been thinking."

"Would not you be thinking the same thing?"

They were staring at the crowd, which included Matt and Tess under a similar archway across the room, and Max, who was standing next to them sipping a drink.

"Yes," Chris said, "but you must not."

"Why? He's here. I feel it is inevitable that I kill him. It is my fate."

"He is heavily guarded. You would be detected, captured and interrogated. You will not last long under interrogation. You will implicate me. This cannot happen."

"So he goes unpunished. Again. He stays alive and happy."

"I have to have your word."

"That's all? Just my word?"

"Yes."

Anna sighed. "You will not let Matt help me?"

"No."

"What about you? You could do it."

"I need your word."

"So be it. You have my word."

"Thank you. And please, Anna, don't fret. I will take care of Dravic."

37.

Prague, September 11, 2012, 10:00 a.m.

"I spoke to Christina," Anna said, "while you were in the shower."

"On Skopelos?" Matt replied.

"Yes."

"Is everything okay?"

"Yes. She said the children were on the beach with Michaela. She is one of the servants, yes?"

"Yes."

"Is she young?"

"In her twenties."

"Does she speak English?"

"Yes."

"Do you know her?"

"Not well, but if Christina hired her, there is nothing else to know about her."

Anna nodded. They were sitting at an outdoor café on the perimeter of Old Town Square, watching the people streaming by under a blue sky. A few clouds high above drifted westward, making their way from Moscow to London. A teacher was standing, talking to a high school class sitting on the ground in front of the equestrian statue in the center of the square.

"What are you thinking, Anna?" Matt asked.

"It cannot be, Teo."

"Anna..."

Anna turned away from the picture-perfect scene before her and looked at Matt, tears in her eyes.

"It cannot be," she repeated.

"Anna. I thought we went through all this."

"You think love is enough, Teo, but it's not. It's not enough."

"Last night it was enough."

Anna said nothing. Tears were streaming down her face. She picked up the linen napkin on the small table and wiped them away. More came, which she ignored. To have found love and to have to give it up, this was a reason to cry. Could she do it?

"We'll get the kids and come back here," Matt said. "Like we said last night."

"Teo. It cannot be."

"Yes, it can," Matt said. "And it will."

38.

Moscow, September 11, 2012, 2:30 p.m.
(Prague, 11:30 a.m.)

The plaster on the walls and ceiling of the passage-
way that ran underground from the Kremlin to Christ
The Savior Cathedral was perhaps two hundred years
old and the thickness of a man's outstretched arm. This
plaster was laid on a succession of hand-made laths
that only an archeologist would find interesting. Not-
withstanding the mocha-colored streaks at random
intervals that revealed areas of poor workmanship or
poor-quality gypsum, it was a complete barrier to all
sound from the world above. A person not accustomed
to the silence could easily be startled by the sound of
his own breath exiting his nostrils. The main corridor
was paved with smooth gray limestone quarried in the
nineteenth century. A footstep on one of these ancient
blocks could be heard a hundred yards away. Naked

bulbs in wire cages on the ceiling threw off the dimmest of light. Narrow side passages intersected the central tunnel every hundred feet or so. These were completely dark. At one of these intersections stood, one on each side of the main artery, two young men in the black, narrow-sleeved cassocks and black, two-buttoned dog collars of Russian Orthodox priests. A third, similarly dressed, sat with Father Nicolei Petrov in his small study, a nine-millimeter pistol aimed at his abdomen.

The two priests had removed the simple components of short-barreled AK 47s from the briefcases they carried, screwed them together, and stood, their backs against their respective walls, weapons loaded and held at their chests, waiting for the sound of the Wolf's footsteps.

39.

Ephesus, September 11, 2012, 11:00 a.m.
(Prague, 12:00 p.m,)

Behind Elias Vasiliou was the crumbling stone
foundation, perhaps two feet high, of a long abandoned
shepherd's cottage. Behind this decaying stonework lay
the bodies of two men, both sharpshooters who had
never even unslung their rifles. Elias had fifteen minutes ago slit the throat of the first and five minutes ago
the second. In the scope of his long-range rifle he now
had Don Viktor Marchenko's head. He could not wait
long. There would be other guards. They would have
two-way radios as the two on the ground did. They
would be checking in and moving this way if there was
no response. Elias had not yet heard the staccato buzz
indicating someone was trying to make contact. When
he did, that would mean they would be coming. *You
may die*, his father had said.

Marchenko had not moved. He was not sleeping. His eyes were open, but he sat as still as a perched hawk searching the ground for prey. The rifle's laser-guided rangefinder read 1802 yards. A mile plus. At the school in Idaho where Elias had trained in long range shooting, he had hit targets at two miles. He was nineteen then and his eyesight had deteriorated slightly since—perhaps it was now twenty-sixteen instead of twenty-fifteen—but his hands were rock steady, as was the rifle as it rested on its matte-finished platinum alloy bi-pod. The rifle's wind velocity meter read SSE/5k. Elias hoped it wouldn't change. If he missed, he would try again, but then, successful or not, he would almost certainly die, as the first thing Marchenko's people would do would be to seal off all exit routes, first and foremost the sea. He looked at his watch: noon. In a second or two the cell phone in his breast pocket would tell him what to do: one buzz, yes, two buzzes, no. Then he returned his cheek to the rifle's smooth barrel and his right eye to its twenty-five-thousand-dollar German-made sight, making sure that the old man's right temple was still in his crosshairs and the wind the same. He knew in his bones that it would be one buzz, that in a few seconds Marchenko's head would be severed from his body, and he would be scampering like a goat down to the launch that was tied up behind some rocks in a cove along the beach below.

40.

Prague, September 11, 2012, 12:00 p.m.

The triple-paned wall-to-ceiling windows in Chris's penthouse were not just bulletproof. The inner pane contained an electro-magnetic barrier against any and all parabolic listening technology. The outer pane was black to the exterior eye. In addition, Chris's devices—his cell phone, his tablet and his laptop—contained "architecture" that, according to Max and Mr. White, guaranteed that any data he transmitted or received was encrypted "everywhere at all layers of the technology stack." "We can't send smoke signals," Max had said. "We have to be able to communicate instantly and with one-hundred-percent reliability. Assuming everything else is equal, which I don't, that's where the edge is. We're listening to them and they're listening to us all the time." Chris would prefer to convey important information in person, the way the old-school Mafia dons and their underlings did. *Search, drink wine or annisette, talk.* Then people died or made fortunes.

He had thus, moments ago, spoken carefully but openly with Costa in Athens.

"He entered the cathedral a few moments ago," Costa had said.

"Your men?"

"Two young priests are doing research in the passages. Your new friend has been very helpful."

"They have the description?"

"Yes, he looks like a wolf."

"He will have security."

"They will all die."

"And our friend in Turkey?"

"He is in his grotto."

"Your man is in place?"

"Yes."

"Go ahead. Call me when they're both dead."

"Of course, Nonos. And Dravic?"

"Let him go. I have other plans for him."

Chris looked at his watch. Noon. The ceremony in Wenceslas Square would be starting soon. Tess and Anna were down in the square. He knew he would not be able to see them but he looked anyway. A beautiful day, the atmosphere festive, many happy people waiting to see President Klaus and Secretary Clinton. Security would still be very high but, now that the Vinice Towers had been raided, the risk of an attack very low. Chris looked at his watch again. Twelve-ten. *Was* the risk low? Nervous, feeling not quite at ease, he pulled a thick manila folder out of his desk drawer. It contained Stefan Kovarik's surveillance file. He had looked through it before, read the reports, scrutinized the photographs. He decided to look at the pictures again. Over a hundred were taken at various times of the people entering and leaving the hi-rise. About half way through, he came across one of a handsome young man with long black hair entering the building. On his arm was a pretty blonde. *That hair.* Then he took his cell phone out of his shirt pocket, opened up its images folder and began scrolling. He stopped at the close-up of a handsome young man with long black hair at the helm of a skiff, smiling widely into the camera: *Tess's cell phone camera. Patriki*, he said out loud, and then he heard an explosion in the square below.

41.

Prague, September 11, 2012, 12:00 p.m.

"You look sad," Tess said. "Are you okay?"

"It's Teo," Anna said.

"Matt? You call him Teo?"

"Yes, he told me about your Uncle Teo, who was gay."

Tess smiled at the memory, but then noticed the tears in Anna's eyes.

"What is it?"

"I am ten years older than him. I have two children by another man."

Tess did not respond. Of course these thoughts had entered her mind as well. The clichés were comforting and had made her feel wise. *Older women clung to younger men. It would have to end. She will get hurt. Love hurts.*

"I have tried to tell him," Anna said, "but he won't listen."

"Tell him what?"

"That he has his life before him. That we must end it."

"Anna..." This scenario Tess had not envisioned, and now she felt smaller, and foolish, the price one pays for prejudging the hearts of others.

"He must have a proper marriage," Anna said, "children of his own."

Silence.

"Have you ever had to break up with someone you love, Tess?"

"No."

"He will not take no for an answer, and I am weak."

"You love him."

"Yes, of course."

"What will you do?" Tess asked.

"I am thinking of staying here, of bringing the children here."

"Have you told Matt?"

"Yes."

"What does he say?"

"He says he will stay with me, that he will never leave me."

"He can be stubborn, Anna. Maybe..."

"Yes. Maybe?"

"Maybe you should give it a chance."

"You cannot decide for me, Tess."

"I know that."

"My heart is aching."

Tess reached across the table and took one of Anna's hands in hers. No family, Tess thought, no money, two kids, on her own, bleakness, and yet she's trying to do the right thing. What is the right thing?

"We can be sisters," Tess said. "No matter what."

Anna smiled at this and squeezed Tess's hand hard before letting go of it.

They were seated at a sidewalk table at a café on the north side of Vaclavske Namesti. Up and down the avenue the outdoor tables of cafés and restaurants were filled with people talking and sipping after-lunch coffee and tea. The tree-lined avenue, its center dotted with small oases of green, was in its full splendor under a cloudless blue sky, the day warm, the breeze cool and gentle. To the west Anna and Tess had a direct view of the wooden barriers that had been set up to block access to Wenceslas Square, creating a hundred-foot buffer around the equestrian statue of the patron saint of the Czech state. Czech special forces soldiers, machine guns slung across their chests, stood guard along the waist-high wooden barrier every twenty feet or so. Behind them there was another hundred feet of empty space and beyond that the rows of chairs for the dignitaries who would be attending the ribbon cutting for the renovation of the National Museum. The dais, which had been built in front of St. Wenceslas on his trotting horse, was empty, but the seats surrounding it were beginning to fill.

A movement among the tables of the café next door, a pub where college students and young travelers were drinking beer in the bright sunlight, caught Tess's eye. Looking over, she saw a tall and pretty blonde girl hugging and kissing a young man with lustrous long black hair. The people at the tables nearby clapped their hands and one or two whistled. The girl held a bouquet of pink flowers in her hands as she clasped them on the young man's back. When they broke from their embrace the man walked away but stopped and turned to wave goodbye to the woman before reaching the edge of the square. He was wearing a bright yellow card around his neck with numbers on it. Tess wondered for a moment what this was but then dismissed the thought.

"They have placed an American flag on St. Wenceslas's staff," Anna said, pointing to the statue.

Tess looked and saw the small American flag waving at the tip of the metal staff the saint carried in his right hand. "So they have," she said, smiling.

The commotion caused by the two young lovers at the pub had subsided and now all eyes were turning toward St. Wenceslas as the dais was beginning to fill with government and museum officials. All of them had entered from the museum itself, as had all of the guests in the seats below. They were all wearing yellow cards around their necks. The last two on the dais were Czech president Vaclav Klaus and United States Secretary of State Hillary Clinton.

"My father says Clinton is here to strong-arm Klaus," said Tess.

"Strong-arm him to do what?"

"To be more Euro-friendly."

"I hope he resists," Anna said.

"Why?"

"They will enslave us again."

"Anna..."

"Look at this," said Anna, her voice suddenly tense, showing Tess a video on her cell phone's screen. "They are storming the American embassy in Cairo."

Anna and Tess put their heads closer to the tiny device and watched, their eyes darting from the pictures of a building on fire, under siege by a mob, to the news crawl at the bottom: *American ambassador, three others killed in Benghazi.* Tess's eyes were riveted on the mob, all young, rabid Arab men, their eyes blazing with hate, and then she remembered the young man with the long black hair as he turned to wave goodbye to the blonde woman. *Patriki.* She looked toward the square and there he was walking toward the barrier, waving to a soldier and pointing to his yellow card, lifting it for the soldier to see. Tess could see the soldier hesitate. *Should he leave his post? Who was this guy?*

Without thought, Tess rose and headed after him.

∧ ∧ ∧ ∧ ∧

Startled, Anna rose to look after her new sister. *Patriki,* she heard Tess call out at the top of her voice. But the dark-haired young man did not turn. Who was this Patriki, Anna said to herself, half smiling, a former boyfriend? Then she remembered seeing the woman Patriki was hugging slip something into his jacket pocket. A love note, she thought at the time, but it was metallic, she now recalled, something hard. A gun? Tess was running now, calling, "Patriki, wait!"

Anna leapt over the café's railing. Ahead Tess was closing on Patriki. They were about twenty feet from the barrier. Running faster than she could have imagined possible, Anna saw Tess grab Patriki by the shoulder, saw him shake her off, turn quickly and slam a closed fist into her face, knocking her flat to the ground, saw the soldier approaching, unslinging his rifle. Anna sped up and leaped on Patriki's back. They went down, and Anna thought, how wonderful, my heart feels so light, how could this be? She did not hear the explosion, or feel it.

But the people nearby did, watching in horror as it scattered Anna and Patriki and the soldier in many bloody directions.

42.

Ruzyne Airport, Prague,
September 11, 2012, 10:00 p.m.

"You have friends in high places," said Stefan Kovarik.

"I told you we'd be leaving," Chris Massi replied.

"When can I speak again with your daughter?"

"Soon. But she's told you all she knows. She thinks the blonde slipped something into Patriki's pocket, the flowers were a shield."

"The girl is on the loose."

Chris did not reply immediately. They were standing on the tarmac, Chris's jet idling thirty yards away. Czech Special Forces troops were guarding the high chain-link fence that enclosed this section of the airport, which was closed, except for patrolling soldiers and military dogs. His would be the only flight out of Ruzyne tonight. "Tess never saw her face," he said, finally.

"Still."

"Soon. I'll call you. Can you come to Skopelos?"

"Of course."

"We were lucky."

Kovarik nodded.

"I have something for you," Chris said.

"What?"

Chris handed the Czech agent a piece of notepaper. "It's a GPS tracking signal."

"Tracking *what*?"

"A yacht. *The Frie Markit*. You can pick up Mr. Dravnova whenever you want."

Kovarik smiled.

"Be careful," Chris said. "He's guarded."

"We will be."

"And my son's here. You have his number."

"Yes."

"He'll bring Anna's body to Skopelos."

"She came home to die, I'm afraid."

Chris nodded. "I think she knew it, somehow."

"And her children? They are Czech citizens as well as American."

"I'll take care of them."

EPILOGUE

Skopelos, September 17, 2012, 6:00 p.m.

From his seat on the rear balcony of his house in Skopelos, Chris could see Christina and two of the house maids setting the table under the grape arbor situated on a flat piece of ground at the foot of his olive grove. The slanting rays of the setting sun filled the rear of the property with a golden light. Behind the arbor a gravel path led down to the small cemetery where this morning they had buried Anna Cervenka. Christina, who had insisted on being the one to tell Anna's children that their mother was dead, had fingered her prayer beads throughout the graveside service, murmuring the Greek Orthodox Jesus Prayer, once for each of the hundred beads, in thick island Greek. Anna was the mother of the Virgin Mary, she had said to Chris when the service was over and she had placed her beads on top of the casket. *A great saint.* Then she went back to her many duties, which now included raising Antonin and Franka, Anna's children, who had been told they would be with Christina for a few days but would now be with her much longer.

Chris had asked Tess and Matt to join him for a drink at six, and saw them now coming onto the stone terrace through the living room's tall French doors. They approached and sat facing Chris across a round, wrought iron coffee table that was covered with a snowy white tablecloth and set with crystal rocks glasses, small white china plates and silverware. Tess and Matt were followed by another house servant, a new one, who was hired to help Christina with Antonin and Franka. She carried an inlaid tray containing an ice bucket, a bottle of Johnnie Walker Black, and a bowl of black olives, which she placed on the table.

While Chris was placing two ice cubes in each glass and pouring the whisky, Matt turned to the new young servant. "Where are the children, Katerina?"

"They are being bathed."

"By who?"

"Michaela."

"Why not you?"

"The staff, they love these children. Shall I...?"

"No, but please bring them down when they're done."

"I will."

Chris raised his glass as Katerina walked away. Matt and Tess did the same. Chris, his glass poised in midair, nodded to his children but said nothing.

"To what?" Tess said.

"You tell me."

"To you," she said.

"To Anna," said Matt.

They clinked glasses and took sips.

"What happened, Dad?" Tess said.

"Fourteen people died," Chris replied.

"Who?"

"A woman in Moscow named Irina Tabak was the first."

"Who was she?" Matt asked.

"Nobody. Someone framed for stealing diamonds that were never stolen."

"Never stolen?" Matt said.

"The GRU probably has them, but set her up for it. Your friend Nico killed her."

"And the other thirteen?" Tess asked.

"Captain Stavros of the Scorpion, the two that Max killed in Brighton Beach, Skip Cavanagh, four Chechan terrorists in Prague; Patriki, Anna, the Czech soldier; a Russian don named Marchenko, a Russian spy master called the Wolf."

"What about Nico and Natalya?" Matt asked.

"They're alive, in Warsaw."

"Why?"

"They weren't spies, just thugs, idiots. They may be useful."

"What happened?" Tess asked.

"Can *you* tell *me*?"

"No, I'm lost."

"Matt?"

Matt shook his head.

"How's your nose?" Chris said to Tess. Her bandages had been removed just the day before; her eyes were discolored but the swelling had gone down.

"Fine."

"I was careless," Chris said.

"No you weren't," said Tess.

"How?" Matt asked.

"I assumed that Patriki was killed by Dravic. I barely looked at the picture Tess sent me."

"Am I still going to Arizona?" Tess asked.

"Yes. You'll know what to do the next time someone takes a wild swing at you."

Father and daughter smiled at each other.

"What happened?" Matt asked.

"The attack in Prague was supposed to line up with the ones in the Middle East. It would have been a disaster, Hillary Clinton killed, the Czech president. The Wolf tried his best to implicate me in it, starting with the money we paid for the diamonds, *if* we bought the diamonds."

"Why? Who *are* you, Dad?" Tess asked.

"I'm a weapon," Chris answered.

"A weapon?" Tess said.

"That's what it comes down to," said Chris.

"Dad..."

"We'll talk later," Chris said. "Here come the kids."

Michaela was standing just inside the French doors, one child in each hand. Bathed in sunlight, they were beautiful children, the girl, five, dark like her father, and the boy, four, blond like his mother. They were composed, but somehow tense, like child actors about to go on stage. They have their role now, Chris thought. Then he looked over at Matt, who was staring with great intensity at the children.

"We'll take care of them, Matt," Chris said. "They're part of our family now."

"What about Dravic?" Matt asked.

"The Czechs have him. They're going to try him for the torture and murder of Antonin Cervenka."

"Do they have the death penalty in the Czech Republic?" Matt asked.

"No," Chris replied.

Matt nodded, his eyes flat, expressionless.

"What are you thinking?" Chris asked.

"Inevitability," Matt replied. Then, smiling, the children approaching, he picked up his glass of scotch and said, "To Anna, and the debt we owe her."

About the Author

James LePore is an attorney who has practiced law for more than two decades. He is also an accomplished photographer. He lives in South Salem, NY with his wife, artist Karen Chandler. He is the author of four other novels, *A World I Never Made*, *Blood of My Brother*, *Sons and Princes*, and *Gods and Fathers*, as well as a collection of three short stories, *Anyone Can Die*. You can visit him at his website, www.jamesleporefiction. com.

A Note from the Author

The Mafia myth in American culture first coalesced in 1972 around the movie *The Godfather*, a portrayal that was on the whole more positive than negative, Don Corleone as Robin Hood you might say. Things got darker in *The Godfather II* in 1974, darker still with the release of *Goodfellas* in 1990, and darkest of all in the television series *The Sopranos*, debuting in 1999. Despite all this utter blackness—the insane violence, the degradation of women, the venality and corruption of public officials—the myth continues to fascinate us. In the Mafia world as we see it—perhaps I should say as I see it—the stakes and the means of achieving them are medieval in nature. Kings, queens, princes, bastard heirs, all battle for power, wealth and turf, the very stuff that land is made of, a piece of the earth itself. Kings and princes, some good, some evil, some on a journey to one or the other, all fighting for realms, will always fascinate us.

Sons and Princes, the novel from which *The Fifth Man* grew, was my homage to the Mafia myth as seen through the eyes of one man, the honorable, decent, very smart and ultimately very brave Chris Massi. At the end of *Sons and Princes*, Chris had a choice to make, and now you know how he chose. To me, who created him, this is the only choice he could have made. It was pre-ordained. He is now a weapon, a weapon that his country will wield again in future novels as Chris's destiny, and America's, continue to unfold.

James LePore
South Salem, New York
December, 2012